cope

Copyright © 2012 by Gabriel Blackwell
All rights reserved.
CCM Design & Cover by Michael J Seidlinger
ISBN – 978-1-937865-02-3

For more information, find CCM at:
http://copingmechanisms.net

SHADOW MAN: A BIOGRAPHY OF LEWIS MILES ARCHER

EDITED BY
Gabriel Blackwell

EADEM MUTATA RESURGO
-epitaph, Jakob Bernoulli's tombstone

EADEM MUTATA RESURGO
-motto, College de 'pataphysique

AUTHOR'S NOTE

The truth is this world is full of no-name Joes, guys with names that mean bunk, and toes tagged with John Doe in every morgue in every city in every country.

Some Johns are born without names. Some have their names taken away by circumstance. Some have names so sorry they can't wait to get down to the courthouse to change them and some have so many names you couldn't say which was which, and you wouldn't want to anyway. They'd just give you a new one, and then where would you be? I mean it isn't the name that's important. But sometimes the name is all you've got to go on. And as the man says, you've got to go on.

There are enough names in this book to fill a Chinatown directory, but that's history for you. The suckers out there might stumble a few times, but it can't be helped.

SHADOW MAN

[1]

Lewis Miles Archer, or anyhow the man known to creditors and clients as Lewis Miles Archer for just long enough to build up a respectable sheet of both, was born sometime between 1879 and 1888, somewhere in the shadow of Lake Michigan. That's a hole wide enough for a boxcar full of babies to fall through, sure, but then the first time that that name, "Lewis Miles Archer," rears its salt-and-pepper head in the public record isn't until 1928, a full forty years later, and on the West Coast. Like a tramp holding two pieces of bread and praying for cheese, it would be nice to have something to put there in between, but the man's history before 1928 is like wet tissue paper—try to pick it up and watch it disappear.

In those forty-odd years, this great nation was dragged into the Great War and then managed to drag itself into the Great Mistake,

Prohibition. It's hard to know which was worse; at least we could blame someone else for the war. We elected a Roosevelt twice, a Coolidge once, and a Debs not at all, which didn't stop the man from trying four times. The Chicago White Sox dyed their footwear black for a season, the Bums from Brooklyn couldn't buy a World Series, and the Red Sox sold the greatest player in the game for a box of cigars and a play called *My Lady Friends*. The boardwalks of America went from sawdust and nickelodeons to Al Jolson and *Lights of New York*, while the airstrips went from Wilbur and Orville to Charles and Amelia. Things changed from day to day, and people learned to keep up, or else they didn't. The ones that didn't were called "suckers."

Lewis Miles Archer's birth doesn't feature in any of the history books, but sometimes the suckers write books, too. In 1879, a boy named John Macdonald Millar was born in Kitchener, Ontario to a family of Scots. Another boy, Raymond Thornton Chandler, was born just a few hours away, in Chicago, Illinois, in 1888. Samuel Dashiell Hammett was born a few years later still, in 1894, in Maryland. Somewhere in between, our boy, Archer, breathed his first; at least, that's the best guess anybody's come up with so far. All four men, Hammett, Millar, Chandler and Archer, would be in San Francisco by the time the lanterns got hung out on Market Street to celebrate the ringing in of 1928. Only Hammett would be left when those lanterns went back up to herald 1929.

In that year, "Archer Investigations" is listed in the San Francisco directory at 111 Sutter Street, the Hunter-Dulin Building. It would be gone before the year was up, replaced by an insurance outfit, "L.D. Walgreen's Family Insurance Company." The tea leaves of public documents from that single year, 1928, are the only solid evidence that the man existed at all, and even there, there aren't that many clues as to the man he was. There is no "Archer, Lewis Miles" listed in any of the city directories from that year or any other, and Archer's name appears only twice in the public record: once on a marriage certificate, and once on the business lease of the office space on Sutter. Back then, all you needed was a signature and ready cash, and you were in business. Archer had a signature and ready cash, and Archer Investigations was in business.

[2]

Archer's partner at Archer Investigations was a wormy little former Pinkerton suffering from a serious case of tuberculosis. Dashiell Hammett's lungs kept him away from the Western Front and in stateside Army hospitals during the war, and those same lungs were now keeping him off the streets and in a desk chair. He had left the Pinkertons in August of 1927, and was just barely scraping by on a 50% disability pension from the Army while looking for work in the bottom of a rye bottle. That meant that his previous life, living high on the hog in an SRO in the city while his wife and kids treaded water in a bungalow across the bay, was over, unless he found gainful employment but quick. Hammett should have been more appreciative—Archer's offer saved the gaunt gigolo from having to bunk with the old ball and chain. But Hammett was Hammett; he paid

Archer back by sleeping with his wife, or trying to, anyway. Some guys.

Hammett's path west from Maryland was typical of the Pinkerton ops working the West Coast beats, and probably similar to the one Archer had followed on his own trip west of the West. It was a yellow brick road paved with conmen and robber barons, stretching all the way out to the goldfields of the Sierra Nevadas and finally dead-ending in the bayside dives of old San Francisco.

Back in the Gold Rush days, prospectors who took the slow boat around the Isthmus of Panama to The City by the Bay were called Argonauts, desperate men much more likely to find themselves fleeced than Golden. The trip was long and dangerous, by sea or overland, and the chances of making a fortune didn't change with the scenery: the conmen's faces, on the other hand, and the shell-games they ran on the suckers, did. But there were enough get-rich-quick schemers in America to fill a continent and they kept pouring over the mountain passes and through the busy ports, long after the fields had dried up. Their sons and grandsons were second- and third-generation schemers, better than their fathers and grandfathers at scheming but no better at business, and a lot more desperate from decades of bread and water in the land of plenty. California was the land of sunshine, the short-con, and the easy sucker, and all that litter on the road to paradise made

Allan Pinkerton and his sons rich, picking up the greenbacks of the Western fatcats on the backs of their operatives in the field.

Still, for real square pegs like Hammett, life as a Pinkerton nobody was better than a stack of society pages and a bellyful of caviar. No other profession could have dragged the son of Dick Hammett from the ruined estate in rural Maryland where he ate dirt as often as doughnuts, through the grease- and coal-stained labor dens of Chicago and the Upper Midwest, all the way to the shanghais and silk suits of San Francisco.

The Hammetts were the oldest family in Hammettville, and the crookedest. Dick Hammett, Dashiell's father, kept his can of striped paint ready for any stroller in Hammettville stupid enough to flash walking money, but his real passion was dames. His tally of affairs outpaced even his resume, nothing to sneeze at even with a cold. He had managed to keep pace with his boy's age, holding seventeen different jobs by the time that Hammett left home at seventeen, even stooping to run for public office, twice. A Pinkerton sleuth came through to check up on Dick's political ambitions at the urging of his Democratic opponent, and Hammett, lured by an honest buck and a chance to get one over on his father, signed on as an informant. The Agency took him on and he spent the next several years working his way across the country as a nutcracker.

As a rookie Pinkerton, Hammett was mostly used as leverage to crack hard union nuts who kept pushing the big con that every man had a right to life, liberty, and the pursuit of happiness, all while feeding his family and even seeing them once in a while. Hammett knew better—his father was at least a good teacher. Pinkerton road agents in the West picked up their checks by flexing muscle for flabby bigwigs who owned mines or railroads, or both. To look at pictures of the young Hammett, you would never finger the boy for a Pinkerton—at just over six feet and shy of 160 pounds, he had about as much muscle as one of the bigwigs, without the wig, and without the fat head. Hammett had brains, at least, but mostly he kept them in his back pocket for later.

When America entered the war in 1918, Hammett entered the Army, bluffing his way past the physical only to get hung up before he ever saw combat. His tuberculosis flared up during a training exercise, and the tell-tale crimson scarf got him admitted to United States Public Health Service Hospital Number 59, the Army hospital in Tacoma, Washington. He never even left the West Coast. Instead, he and his tubercular buddies yo-yoed from Tacoma to San Diego and back again, Army hospital to Army hospital, spending weekends in Seattle or Los Angeles, drinking rye, playing cards, and swatting white-coated tail whenever it came close enough. He even met his future wife, Josephine "Jose" Dolan, an Army nurse, while at Hospital Number 59.

The Army gave Hammett the heave-ho when he could keep the coughing quieter than a sea lion in heat, and, with Jose pregnant, the two followed the Pinkerton dough to San Francisco, where everything went sour. But not before the Hammetts had signed on the dotted line to see each other through sickness and health, until death do them part. Two daughters and two jobs later, the famous fog had jimmied its way into Hammett's chest and set up house, and Jose and the girls were moved across the bay to keep them from getting Hammett's TB. Or so he said. It was a rich set-up for a pimp like Hammett, but it meant that he had two roofs to keep over his head. Even a 100% disability pension couldn't help him there. He needed something with meat on it to avoid starvation, or, even worse, moving back in with his family. Any job that would keep Hammett in sour mash and salesgirls would do. Archer had just the spot for him.

[3]

Working for the Pinkertons had been half adventure story, half civil service exam: for every lead that had to be followed up out in the streets, there was a sheaf of paperwork waiting back at the office, dull as a butter knife and not nearly as shiny. At Archer Investigations, with Hammett chained to a desk on Sutter, Archer was finally free to work the shoe-leather full time as an investigator and shadow man.

The shadow man, a younger, ambulatory Hammett had written to Jose from his first post-hospital Pinkerton posting in Spokane, Washington, "is meant to blend in, to disappear by being always there. It does you no good to hide yourself, because then . . . the guy you're shadowing . . . if he notices you, he notices you trying to hide from him." Later, in a story he called "Zigzags of Treachery," he posted the clubhouse rules: get behind your man and stay there, don't try to hide from your man or he'll get suspicious, act like you're supposed to be there doing whatever it is you're doing and nothing else, and don't ever look your man in the eye. Suspicion might be raised, Hammett must have felt it went without saying to his former nurse, if the shadow man were huffing, puffing, and coughing all of the time because of San Francisco's famous hills; you had to keep up with the man you were following, after all.

Hammett was on a strict diet of recirculated air and relaxation, laid up behind his desk with nothing but a bottle and his memories to keep him company. He handled the clients and decided where to send Archer when. He could do a few things on the phone or at City Hall or the library, but working the streets was out. Archer turned in his field reports and Hammett prettied them up to suit himself, the clients, and posterity. Of course, this means that what little is left from the days of Archer Investigations is in Hammett's slanted handwriting. Hammett had a penchant for exaggeration, inherited from the old man, but it was only exaggeration, not outright lying. Mostly, he embellished because he couldn't be there himself. You might see a lot from behind a desk, but you'll miss some things. Hammett sure did.

Hammett was meticulous enough to keep the doors open when it came to the records that had to be filed with the D. A. or the P. D.—it was his job, after all, the real reason that Archer kept him around—but he was pretty sloppy when it came to the day-to-day of the agency. No one ever said that Hammett was good at his job, just that he did it. All but the last few of Archer's field reports have gone missing, and the client reports, the ones that Hammett would have written, are a tangle of conjecture and coincidence, like a dime novel you paid two bits for. Hammett couldn't be bothered to do the real work of putting a case together—he spent his days upending bottom-drawer bottles or throwing pennies out the window to see if they'd come back dollars. He wasn't much of a detective when he was sitting on his brains.

[4]

Archer was the senior man—he had his name on the door, after all—but Hammett's ego, and the fact that it was his hand holding the pen, turned "Archer Investigations" into "Spade and Archer," with Hammett just barely hiding that bulky ego behind Spade's John Hancock. In Hammett's *The Maltese Falcon*, published by Alfred A. Knopf in 1930, "Sam Spade"—read Samuel Hammett—eventually finds the person who murdered "Miles Archer" back in the first chapter, and recovers the falcon in question in the process. Quite a hero, for a guy who only left his desk to go to the bathroom or the speak downstairs.

Never mind that most of the cases that Archer Investigations handled were the standard insurance company closed-purse accounts, and the occasional jealous husband jealous wife, or the hood with something to hide and nowhere to put it. The pair did well enough: Hammett kept himself in whiskey and white-stocking dancehall graduates, and Archer brought home a former Ziegfeld girl at least twelve years his junior, used to riding the high horse and damn good at it, too.

Iva Goodbody, born Penelope Sampson, danced the hoochie-koo a few nights a week in one of the upscale joints on the fringes of what used to be the old Barbary Coast until the ink dried on the marriage certificate. Dancers like Goodbody retire at forty—their looks retire before then. The smart ones keep the money they make hustling, and lean on gentlemen Johns for everything else. Goodbody was a smart one.

She was evidently still living up to her name when she became Mrs. Lewis Miles Archer: in *The Maltese Falcon*, Hammett tried to write himself into her pants. But, back in the real world, there were no indications that Goodbody wasn't keeping up her subscription to *Good Housekeeping*.

As Penelope Sampson, Goodbody was a local girl, or near enough for the West, from the tiny ranch town of Santa Teresa, about 300 miles down the coast from San Francisco. She had gone east to make it in showbiz, but somewhere along the Hudson, the Big Bad Wolf busted her rose-colored glasses. She had been cursed with gams like parsnips, a chest like a bowling alley ball return, curly red locks, and eyes like the Pacific on a clear day. Men couldn't see past all that rich splendor, or didn't care to, and she bounced around as a model for a little while before getting a hand up into the Ziegfelds and then striking out on her own, back West. In a June 2, 1927 note, Goodbody, still Penny Sampson to her father, writes: "Dear Daddy, There are enough hucksters here already. One more would hardly tip the scales, and one less wouldn't make enough of a difference. Maybe I'll take Mr. Greeley's advice after all. I'm going to visit Pearl for a couple of weeks around Christmas, and then maybe I'll take the boat up to Goleta." She did.

Ralph Sampson, Goodbody's father, was a half-time hustler with surprisingly swank connections who spent most of his time doing one hell of a Jay Gatsby impression. Penelope argued with the old man on her return, possibly about the way she was earning her living, maybe about the way he was earning his, and left home again—she thought, for good. She was in San Francisco for less than a month before she married Archer.

The marriage certificate gives the date of the Archers' wedding as January 21, 1928. The witnesses are Dashiell and Jose Hammett and John and Annie Millar. Archer gives his full name as "Lewis Miles Archer" and lists his birthday either as December 3 or 13, with the one and the last two digits of the birth year rendered illegible by the mimeograph's smudging.

It was a civil ceremony, with a Judge Collinson presiding. In color and atmosphere, not much different from a deposition or a grand jury inquiry, though probably with more salutary, or at least salacious, results.

Hospital records on "Penelope Archer"—the only time that name turns up anywhere—show that she carried a pregnancy to term on February 6 of that year, but there is no accompanying birth certificate, indicating that the child was possibly lost during delivery. No delivery, no invoice: the father's name is written in invisible ink. Mrs. Archer's address is given as 1216 Turk Street, but the *1928 Crocker Langly San Francisco City Directory* has a "Collins, Peter," living at that address.

That same Peter Collins was issued a private investigator's license the previous year, 1927, giving his address as that same 1216 Turk. Lewis Miles Archer was never issued a private investigator's license. Here's the joke, though—"Peter Collins" was the invisible man rousties sent rooks to see when they asked too many dumb questions: "Go see Peter Collins, kid. He'll set you straight."

The man who had pledged his troth to the former Miss Goodbody went looking for Collins and never came back before the couple could even celebrate their first anniversary.

[5]

With most of Archer Investigations' clients in the ground and the files in the trash, even the details of Archer's working life in San Francisco are harder to come by than an honest Cretan. Hammett and Archer spent enough time together in that year to get on each other's nerves, and Hammett always claimed he knew Archer like the lining of his favorite suit, only he didn't look as good, and he itched like the dickens. But he didn't preserve much of that knowledge in writing, unless you count what he put into his novel.

It's a fact that Hammett had his way with the events in the *Falcon*, but it's also a fact that he left enough of the real dirt in so that no one comes out clean, not even Hammett himself. Except for the few pages from Archer's surviving notebook, Hammett's slanted account in *The Maltese Falcon* is most of what's left of the Archer Investigations days. By comparing the field reports and the surviving files with Hammet's "novel," a few of the details can be salvaged as being more or less true, no matter how twisted the mouth that spoke them.

As far as his description of Archer goes, it's all right; he would have had front row seats for that at least, behind the desk at 111 Sutter. Hammett puts Archer's age at "as many years past forty as [Hammett] was past thirty." If Hammett was just turning thirty-four that year, that would put Archer's age at about forty-four, or thereabouts. Could be the man looked old, or looked young. Working backward from that December, Archer's date of birth is either December 3 or December 13, 1879 on through to 1888, maybe even later, though not likely; remember that Hammett himself was born in 1894.

Hammett's few stories about his former partner, most of them in lonely letters to Lillian Hellman from the home in Los Angeles he briefly shared with his wife Jose, indicate that Archer grew up in Chicago but was not, as far as Hammett could tell, born there. His father had been an important man in the U.S. Army, and the family had moved around a lot before they hit Chicago, minus the father. The only physical description of Archer, "five foot ten in stocking feet and solidly built, like half a filing cabinet up on stilts" comes from a typescript of the novel. Hammett would cut out most of that flowery prose before he published the thing; in the meantime, hard-boiled Hammett had gone gaga over a fellow spirit-medium and drinking fountain named Hemingway, who believed in only the tips of icebergs. Of course, that description could serve for either John Macdonald Millar or Raymond Thornton Chandler. But then, it could go for a hundred gees out on the street right now.

As Hammett tells it, "Spade" is the senior man in the agency, and the smart one, the one who's got all the exits covered and the angles bent. The occasion for his story is the case of the Maltese Falcon, walking in the door with a dame whose real name is Brigid O'Shaughnessy, but who hides it under at least two aliases. She also ices Miles Archer, junior partner, and one other man in quick succession, and throws in with Archer's former partner, a dick just wise enough to know not to throw in with her all the way, even if he only figures it out at the very end of the book and fights it even then.

As for that, Hammett never saw a skirt he didn't want to crawl under. He puts the heavy finger on Miles Archer in the novel, but in real life, it was Hammett doing the doctor impersonation at every pair of lashes and curls. If anyone was going to be pulled by a skirt, it was Dashiell Hammett.

And anyway, Archer didn't die. Not by O'Shaughnessy's hand he didn't.

[6]

There is a funny passage in Hammett's novel, one so queer that most people who read it can't forget it, even if they forget most of the rest of the book, easy enough to do. That would include the publisher of the book, Alfred A. Knopf himself, who advised Hammett to forget the passage if he wanted Knopf to go ahead with printing the book. That little passage had nothing to do with the falcon, nothing to do with the "case" that Spade and Archer were supposed to be working on, and it would only pull the reader out of the story, Knopf said. Hammett, though, wouldn't let it go. It was important to him that it be there. Like a big fat hairy mole on a pretty girl's face, it stuck out like a sore thumb, and that was the point for Hammett.

Hammett's spirited mind marked the story of Flitcraft as a distillation of what the rest of the novel was about, a parable almost, important in some way he couldn't quite figure. Knopf thought that this was bullshit of the first order, and he wasn't going to step in it. He wasn't going to let his company step in it either, and he wanted Hammett to shovel it up double-time. Up to this point in their relationship, Hammett had been completely cowed by his publisher, but this time, with the *Falcon* and Flitcraft, Hammett held his ground. Flitcraft stayed in.

In Hammett's telling, Sam Spade tracks down a man, Flitcraft, who has gone missing from his Tacoma, Washington home. Flitcraft is a real estate agent with a wife and two kids. He's happy, the kind of happy that people dream about when they read too many magazines—his business is doing well, he inherited a pile of money from his father, and he plays golf on Sundays when it isn't raining too hard. His kids don't even get into trouble. But then, one day, as he's walking to lunch, a girder falls just inches short of his nose, from four stories up, cracking the pavement and nearly killing him. Turns out he's peachy apart from a scratch on the cheek from the sidewalk chipping, but the experience of nearly signing the deed on the farm gets to him. He realizes he's going to die. Today, tomorrow, someday. So he walks away from it all, everything, his whole life in Tacoma.

It takes him a couple of years to settle back down from that girder's fall, but that's exactly what he does. Turns out the guy just moves a couple of hours away, to Spokane, Washington, where, guess what? He has a wife, two kids, and a successful business—this one, a car dealership. Charles Pierce. Pierce Motors.

Hammett has his Spade tell the story to the femme fatale of his novel, Brigid O'Shaughnessy, but he never explains why. Even O'Shaughnessy asks why. Spade explains that what is so interesting about the case is that the guy, Flitcraft or Pierce, changed his whole life, left everything behind, only to walk right into a mirror image of that life just a few hours away. He got a fresh start, just to wind up back in the same sweaty clothing. But what does that have to do with the falcon?

Hammett admitted he couldn't quite fit it into the novel. Hell, *it was* a sore thumb. He didn't know what the meaning was, really. But he knew it meant something, and he knew he wanted it there. That's all there is to it: just a hint, a clue, a sore thumb. But a sore thumb's only news if you can see the hand that it's attached to. Otherwise, it just looks like a thumb, just like any other thumb. You might even think it was a toe.

One thing you probably wouldn't think was that it was also true.

[7]

In the Pinkerton files of cases Hammett worked on, there is one that matches the Flitcraft episode in almost every particular. After this many years, there are holes in the file big enough to drop a girder through, but what's there makes it even odds that Hammett's little story about Flitcraft is about as fictional as the law of gravity, and a hell of a lot more interesting.

In the file, Hammett gets put on the case of one John Dalmas by the invisible man's wife, Claudine Dalmas, a porcelain statue with lines of glue already showing when she arrives in the Pinkerton offices. She cracks the further the case goes. Hammett eventually tracks the man down, or evidence of the man, in Spokane, going under the name of Stanley Reilly, having remarried. Flitcraft, it seems, was a real gee; Pierce was a real gee. Well, "real" is maybe by this point relative. The point is, Spade isn't just whistling "Dixie" to Brigid O'Shaughnessy. Hammett on his best day couldn't carry a tune in a wheelbarrow.

Page three of the *Tacoma Tribune* of November 19, 1910 reads, "Tacoma Man Missing Now for Two Weeks, Wife Says." The item is smaller than an obituary and just as spare. The wife in question, Claudine Dalmas, gives out the missing man's name as John Dalmas, without specifying his age, according to the reporter. She's cagey, maybe, cagey like a woman about to come into a life insurance payout like every one-armed bandit in Nevada showing fruit all at once. Claudine gives the police and the papers a description of her missing husband, his last known whereabouts, and what he was wearing when he went to work that day, but there isn't room for a photograph of the missing man, or else Claudine doesn't lend the *Tribune* one. Looks an awful lot like Claudine Dalmas doesn't want her husband made. The Pinkertons actually get called in by the insurance company, but can't get a line on Dalmas's whereabouts, and Claudine Dalmas collects. Case notes make it that the Pinkerton principal on the Dalmas case pins Claudine as a serious insurance risk, a widow with no incentive for finding a husband whose disappearance bought her a house on the Sound and a lot of mink, but with the insurance company payout, the file gets closed.

The only reason the Pinkertons get put back on the case years later is that Claudine's son,

John Dalmas, Jr., seven at the time John Senior ducked the girder, turns seventeen and decides his dad isn't dead, or so he tells his mother on his way out the door. He doesn't come home that night, or any other. When a couple of days pass and John, Jr. is still flapping in the breeze, Claudine calls in the Agency.

In Spokane, there's a "Reilly Motor Company," with a business license that runs from 1914-1916, at which point it is turned over to a man named Arthur G. Huck. Huck is the mechanic at Reilly Motors, the first man hired by Stanley Reilly, the Reilly of Reilly Motors. Stanley Reilly, married to Penny Reilly, and proud papa of a baby boy, leaves no records of his life in Spokane prior to 1914, when he buys a home on South Post Street, near where the Davenport Hotel is being put up, and opens his automobile business. There is no mention of any subsequent disappearance, and that's funny, because he seems to stop existing in 1916.

During that time, Hammett sees his last tour of duty in the Army hospital in Tacoma, Washington, and, discharged for good, goes back to his old job at the Pinkerton Detective Agency, which then brings him to Spokane. There are enough open cases at the two offices to sink Hammett's name under the piles of field reports like the *Lusitania* off the coast of Ireland, but this one sticks out.

What goes missing is the name of the principal on the case. Regardless of who does the legwork on a job, every case gets a principal, someone who works directly with the client, because the client never meets the dick doing the legwork. Company policy. Was the principal Archer? There's no way to know, but the case notes read like Archer, with some of the same flavor as Archer's field reports.

The last time Stanley Reilly gets any ink spilled is in Spokane, 1916, to turn over operations of Reilly Motors to Huck "for the duration," indicating that Reilly probably enlisted in the Armed Forces at that time. But that's trouble, too, because none of the branches of the Armed Forces have any record on any Stanley Reilly. Which isn't likely to lift any eyebrows if you consider that the man couldn't have enlisted under that name, anyway, if he had been born John Dalmas. But there's no record of a "John Dalmas," or any other Dalmas, either.

Dalmas, posing as Reilly, serves in some capacity, or maybe just uses the war as an excuse to take yet another powder and never comes back. It's a familiar pattern by now. Maybe another girder falls, or maybe he really does go overseas, and instead of a girder, it's a mortar round. Whatever happens, he doesn't make it back to Penny Reilly and Reilly Motors.

Hammett lucks into a puff of smoke from Dalmas's fire down in San Francisco, courtesy of Claudine Dalmas's sister, Fay, a waitress and sometime dancer there. Reilly had shipped out as a regular seaman under the Dalmas name on the *Jezebel*, a freighter calling Seattle, Washington home and plying the Pacific trade route between San Francisco and Hong Kong. Just under two years later, Stanley Reilly tells his Elks Club cronies that he bought his house and opened Reilly Motors with money made while at sea, on a freighter named *La Paloma*. Thing is, sometime before America entered the war, the *Jezebel* changed its flag and its name, and became *La Paloma*, of Veracruz, Mexico. Of course, neither ship's records list a Stanley Reilly or any other Reilly as shipping out during those years.

Penny Reilly's description of her husband matches Claudine's to a tee, and Penny has a picture, too, which Claudine agrees could definitely be the man, but she won't say one way or the other, probably because of the insurance angle. Apart from that description, there's nothing from the Reilly woman in the file; it's possible that she opened her own case with the Pinkertons after Hammett questioned her about the disappearance of John Dalmas, but if so, that file has been destroyed.

Hammett gets his other big break from Huck, who notices some crooked ink and fancy math in Reilly Motors' books. Hammett then uncovers a few letters in a correspondence file that show that Reilly was making unscheduled trips to San Francisco and Los Angeles before his disappearance. But he gets shut down before he can make any progress in that direction. Claudine Dalmas, maybe spooked by the insurance boys, pulls her financial support, and the file gets closed. The boy's disappearance doesn't get solved under the Dalmas file, but there's more than enough there to connect it to Hammett's retelling fifteen years later in *The Maltese Falcon*.

The question, then, is why Hammett tells the story at all. If Archer was his principal on the case, it might explain their connection as well as the story's reappearance in *The Maltese Falcon*: despite all of the hoopla about the falcon, still a novel about the death of Miles Archer. But it might also suggest that Hammett thought that Archer was taking a page out of his own case files.

[8]

There are only three complete case files left from Archer Investigations, and since none of them paid out much more than a cab fare and a hot plate downtown, we can be sure that they weren't the only three cases Archer and Hammett took on. On the twentieth of February, 1928, Archer Investigations took what looks to be a pro-forma retainer from John Macdonald Millar. Millar hired Archer to look into an infant he found abandoned on the train car on his way into the city that morning. We know that Millar was not really a customer, but more of an agent for Archer Investigations—Millar worked, at the time, as a stringer on the *Los Gatos Mail*, and occasionally provided the agency with information. Not to mention the fact that he was a witness at the Archers' wedding the previous month.

Jack Millar and his wife, Annie, first moved down to San Diego from Vancouver, B.C., at the behest of Annie Millar's sister. Seemed the Millars had been having trouble conceiving, and Annie's sister convinced them that the sunshine would set the stork flying. Sis was a holy roller, as plumped on Jesus as on citrus and sunshine, and the Millars soon found her intolerable, even with the sunshine. They didn't care much for the oranges, either. They moved north, to Los Angeles—still sunny, less Jesus—where they may have met Dashiell Hammett; the time-frame is about right. Something else was right, too: Annie finally got pregnant

But if the sunshine was proving good for the health of the Millars, it did nothing for the health of their baby. It was stillborn. The Millars moved further north, to Santa Teresa.

Millar was the kind of scoop who had ink in his blood: his father, and his father's father before him, were newspapermen, the kind with long, thin fingers, perfect for picking pockets or skittering through files for hours on end. Millar liked to spend his days sweet-talking his way into back rooms doing both, digging up stories the only way he knew how: by following the money. And back in those days, Southern California was a great place for a snoop like Millar. There wasn't a straight municipal official within a stone's throw, and not a one worth throwing the stone. You could get rich just by squinting at the mayor's checkbook. But only if you played the game. Millar didn't like the rules, and kept getting himself in trouble for being on the field without a uniform.

Annie got pregnant again in Santa Teresa. The stork didn't even leave the nest this time—miscarriage, of another baby girl. The couple's doctor in Santa Teresa, Dr. Dwight Troy, told them it might be impossible for them to have children. They kept trying anyway.

Millar was chased out of Santa Teresa by Ralph Sampson's cronies at the District Attorney's office, who forced the local daily to take the pen out of Millar's hand and the food out of his mouth along with it. The Millars headed north yet again, this time to the sleepy San Francisco suburb of Los Gatos.

According to the file, on his way to Archer's office on the intercity, Millar found himself alone in the car with a baby boy on the seat next to him. The baby's mother had been a woman dressed all in black, Millar said, with a black lace shawl, in an interesting pattern that he had noted immediately—like a spider's web, maybe a bit more solid, but unmistakably a spider's web. The woman must have been hiding the baby in her blouse, at her bosom. Millar hadn't seen her face and didn't even know she was carrying a baby. Nor did he see her get up and get off the train: when he realized what had happened, the car was pulling away from the station and Millar was the only rider aboard in the last two rows of seats. That is, if you don't count the baby boy.

Millar approached Hammett and Archer to see what could be done about finding the mother, probably because they were handy, but maybe he had reason to go to them rather than the police.

Archer looked into the northbound line, riding it back and forth to Los Gatos on the lookout for a woman in mourning, while Hammett scoured local hospital records for a boy born in the right time frame and watched the newspapers for any announcements about a missing boy. Meantime, Annie and Jack Millar took care of the infant at their home in Los Gatos. Hammett turned up a couple of decent leads, mothers with their hands out for the state and nutcracker legs for any Joe with two dollars and a full tank of gas, but nothing panned out. All babies accounted for, except for the one at home with the Millars.

Millar himself closed the case, when real work walked in to the Sutter Street office. He couldn't pay for the agency to work it—they had been working on it as a favor to their sometime informant in the downtime between cases—and the agency couldn't afford to turn down a paying customer. Curiously for an upstanding citizen like Millar, there isn't any mention of the baby in the San Francisco Police Department Missing Persons files for February, March, or April 1928.

It doesn't look like either Archer or Hammett made a move to follow up on the foundling after Millar closed the file, and there isn't another word in the files on either the baby or Jack Millar for several months. In between, the Millars announced the birth of a bouncing baby boy in the July 7 edition of the *Los Gatos Mail,* with a celebratory verse by proud papa Jack Millar. Their precocious young son, Kenneth, was walking well before his first birthday. The baby on the train doesn't rate at all.

[9]

The second case to survive the pulp mill doesn't come until December of that year, when the asset-recovery man at the Bank of Montreal, Raymond Chandler, called in Archer Investigations for help with a runaway in pink pantaloons and stiletto high heels passing off-white paper at San Francisco's banks. The case, and everyone involved in it, had to be hushed up so quiet that the mouse loose in the house on Christmas Eve wouldn't have heard it. That case then became the case that Hammett based his novel on, the falcon case. Hammett never was any good at following orders.

Raymond Chandler's position at the bank was as close as he ever got to being a detective. The mug was a peeper all right, but a Tom and not a dick: Chandler preferred not to get his hands dirty in the action, but he sure as hell liked to watch. He liked numbers and words fine, but he hated people and he didn't like to leave the house if he didn't have to.

Chandler had run away up the Coast from the home of his sweetheart in Los Angeles, a woman named Cissy Pascal. Pascal was the happy housewife of Julian Pascal, alias Goodridge Bowen, a piano player and pseudo-intellectual type working for South Basin Oil and heavily in debt to the tweed set running things down at Los Angeles City Hall. Cissy was all set to divorce Pascal and marry Chandler, but Chandler wasn't ready for that; he was still mama's little Ray-Ray, and mama didn't want him settling down with a woman much closer to her age than to Ray-Ray's. He decided to go to San Francisco and wait for the old lady to croak. When she was dead and buried, Cissy and Ray-Ray would be husband and wife. It all happened according to plan, and the couple tied the knot on the fifth of February, 1929. Chandler's life would only barely change; he was just swapping one worn-out horse for another.

Cissy had a checkered past, having started out in New York as an "artist's model" and a taxi dancer, the kind that get paid by the dance, going under the names "Cherry Pearl" and "Cecilia Silver." It's from Cecilia that she got the name that stuck—Cissy—but her real name was Pearl Eugenie Hurlburt. You can see why she changed it.

Julian Pascal was a charity case at South Basin, orphaned in the corner office under a fancy title and a mound of paperwork that would never get done. The man was a piano player, for Christsakes—not too many pianos at South Basin, and even less sheet music. The company was owned by tone-deaf General Norris Sternwood, a close friend of Warren and Alma Lloyd, the couple that Chandler had lived with and worked for—at their Los Angeles Creamery—when he first moved to Los Angeles. The Lloyds and General Sternwood were the crème de la crème of Los Angeles society, and Chandler was only too happy to skim a little off the top. He was smart enough to take only what he could eat right away—cream goes rancid pretty quick out in all that sunshine.

When Chandler chose to cool his carriage up the coast in San Francisco, he left his mailing address care of the Pascals as a little reminder to Pascal that he was still gunning for him. Chandler got his in when the General discovered that Pascal's assistant at South Basin had disappeared with one of the General's check registers and was passing two-bit forgeries around San Francisco like it was the first of the month. Chandler's position at the Bank of Montreal, later the Bank of British North America, tracking down and attempting to recover funds acquired through defrauding the bank, put him in the unique position of being the right man in the right place at the right time. Probably a first for him.

Originally, the General wanted Chandler to handle the deal through his bank, using the bank's dicks to close in on the General's soon-to-be former employee and hand him over to

SFPD. But Chandler discovered a new wrinkle before the net could close, and suddenly, the General wanted the whole thing hush-hush and under the table.

Turned out, Pascal's assistant wasn't alone in the City by the Bay. He was shacking up with the General's youngest daughter, Carmen Sternwood, a hellcat with a lot more scratch than purr. But the General wasn't as liberal with the scratch as his daughter, and while she wasn't on a leash—the old man knew better than that—she didn't have any money to play with when she left the house. So the General didn't want Chandler to snap up the yegg after all—he just wanted his daughter back, safe and sound, where she couldn't do any more damage to his bank account.

Chandler chose Archer Investigations probably on the basis of their size—a small agency like Archer Investigations would have less chance of a leak. But maybe it was just thrift: Archer and Hammett could be bought, part and parcel, for less than the Pinkertons' retainer. They also had the advantage of being a company that Chandler had had no business with in the past and would be unlikely to have business with in the future in the course of his job with the bank.

Chandler presented the case to Hammett as a girl eloping with her boyfriend, and a father who wanted her to know it was all right, just so long as she came home. Archer and Hammett were to get Chandler in touch with the girl, and he would take it from there. The girl, he told

Hammett, was going under the name Carmen Wonderley. Archer would have been out of the office on the case of a man named George Beale, a case whose file was not saved from the wholesale pulping (according to the intake, Beale's wife, Caroline, was seeking his whereabouts, as well as alimony and child support; the client info remains, but any follow-up Archer Investigations did was subsequently destroyed). Chandler didn't know what name the yegg was going under, but he knew where they had been staying—at a flophouse on Geary. That's where the first several checks had been cashed. Chandler had already looked into it; the couple wasn't there anymore.

Hammett took the case and took a look at the checks that Chandler had recovered so far—two from the flophouse, the rest cashed at a branch office of the Bank of America and Italy (shortly thereafter shortened to just "Bank of America," with Il Duce's snatch of the Italian government). Hammett tried to make some sense out of the case for Archer, for when he arrived back at the office, but when five o'clock came and the whistle blew, he got tired of waiting and went home to his two-bit SRO, his nickel cigars and dime novels.

[10]

In *The Maltese Falcon*, it's Miss "Wonderley" that lays out the case, along with two short portraits of Benjamin Franklin—filling Spade in on the elopement and offering to collect the girl and take her back to her parents; in Wonderley's version, her parents, too. Miss Wonderley was looking for her sister, the other Miss Wonderley, or just possibly, she thinks, Mrs. Floyd Thursby, naming the mug that whichever Wonderley wandered off wandered off with. Thursby isn't a right fellow in any telling, not someone you would want your kid sister wandering off with if you cared about your kid sister.

The problem with her story is that there is no second, younger Miss Wonderley—hell, there is no older Miss Wonderley either. There is no "Miss Wonderley" at all—the broad's name is actually Brigid O'Shaughnessy. She poses as

Miss Wonderley to draw Archer out, only to snuff the dick when he gets too close.

Using the chopsticks of Archer Investigations' Chandler/falcon file, along with the few scribblings that are left on the case in Archer's notebook, we can start to pick apart the Angler's loop that Hammett managed to make out of *The Maltese Falcon*.

Chandler visited the office all right, and engaged the services of Archer Investigations. Hammett put in the requisite amount of desk-jockeying that afternoon to get the horse out of the gate, calling around to see what he could get in the way of a physical description on the penman. In the process, he got in touch with a man named Dan Wallace, who had worked the security detail at the Bank of America and Italy for the past month or so.

Wallace didn't have a line on Hammett's forgeries yet, but he promised to take a look. While he had Hammett on the horn, though, Wallace mentioned that he had found out about something, a big deposit, stolen goods likely, destined for the bank vault, that he couldn't talk about over the phone. He wanted to be sure of the deposit's legal status, and he needed help on that end. He told Hammett he wanted to engage Archer Investigations' services, work outside of the bank's security office but still keep it under wraps, if at all possible. Hammett told the boy to come in the next morning, when they could talk it over face to face. That suited Wallace just fine.

Archer was out of the office when Chandler dropped off Miss Wonderley's case and Hammett made the calls. Archer may not have been in the office at all that day, working the walk on George Beale. He was there the next morning, though, when Dan Wallace came around, and Dan Wallace, not knowing what had happened to the guy he talked to on the phone (Hammett was not an early riser, preferring instead to drink late and rise accordingly), played it safe and kept his bottom lip buttoned to his top on the bank business.

Wallace told Archer a tall tale about how he needed muscle, someone who was not affiliated with the bank, for a meeting with a union worker at the docks that night. The errand was supposed to be bank business, but he couldn't talk too much about just what that business was. He tried to request Hammett specifically for the job, saying he knew the man from the Pinkerton's, but Hammett wasn't the muscle in the operation, Archer was. Hammett didn't have enough muscle to knock over a fly in a strong wind. This was only a few years before Bloody Thursday and the riots on the docks, and even in 1928, the stevedores' union wasn't a gang to mess with lightly, or alone. Archer was suspicious—why would someone working security at the Bank of America and Italy need to meet a union man at the docks after dark? Why would a bank dick need muscle? And why ask specifically for the lunger Hammett, if he was looking for muscle?

Archer took the case all the same, not yet knowing he was already supposed to be working the case that Hammett had mistakenly taken home with him overnight, or that Wallace was playing the agency like a violin with only two strings. Archer didn't ask Dan Wallace the right questions because he didn't know there were right questions to ask; Archer Investigations kept its doors open all right, but it wasn't through turning down clients, no matter how bad their stories smelled. When Hammett came in later that day, he found that Archer already had plans for that night, covering Dan Wallace, the bank dick from the bank where the wrong gee from Los Angeles was passing bad checks. Hammett filled his boss in on the Chandler job, and Archer headed out the door before the two could compare notes on Wallace.

Archer rushed to do some of the leg work on the Chandler case, but had to cut it short when the Wallace appointment rolled around. He figured an inside line with Wallace on what his new client knew about the bank's business, so he skipped the Bank of America and Italy, which just happened to be the place where the majority of the checks were cashed and where the tellers might have been able to provide Archer with a physical description of the gee that Chandler was looking for. It was sloppy casework, but sometimes that's all that you have time for. Archer was chasing a scent but already barking up the wrong tree.

From the field notes in Archer's notebook:

The Embarcadero car gets to Pier 9 a little early. Must be my lucky night. Wallace is nowhere to be found. I figure ten minutes to clap an eye on the meeting spot before he's due.

There's a zigzag of stacks of packing crates and luggage from the liner docked at the next pier over, all the way down to the water. It wouldn't be a straight shot even with a Springfield: you can't see the bay end from the land end. The crates go up twelve or fifteen feet, tall enough to drown out the light from the Embarcadero and the Ferry Building and make shadows between stacks big enough to hide an elephant and its daughter in. Or a union man with a chip poking out through his collar thick enough to knock down a circus-tent full of bank dicks. A passing patrolman wouldn't see a thing. Wouldn't hear a thing, either, not over bay traffic on a busy night like this. And there aren't any patrolmen anyway, not on this side of town at this time of day.

With the ship horns calling the sea lions and the sea lions calling the brass section of the Barbary Coast symphony orchestra, I don't hear the voices until I'm just about to round the last stack of crates before a big gap.

Wallace is arguing with some sort of cat, and the cat's winning. I try to get closer, but I can't figure how to get around the last stack of crates—some hand luggage from one of the passenger liners's spilled out into what would have been the aisle, and there's no way to get closer without causing an avalanche and maybe taking a swim. The bay is bound to be cold tonight, and I've got on my heavy wool suit.

I take up a position behind the shortest stack in the row (some kind of building materials, I think, with Chinese stamps, smelling like old leather left out in the rain and then smothered in cinnamon), giving me a sightline and getting me close enough to smell the fish that Wallace's customer—a Chinese national, possibly named "Xu Li" or "Xiu Li" [in the margin, Archer wrote: *Julie? Is Li a dame? Is the Chinese getup just for show? Who's this Li trying to fool, Wallace or me? H: get with the casuals tomorrow, see if you can get a line on this character*]—*ate for dinner. Li is not a stevedore, any more than I'm an organ grinder, and he's definitely not Italian—he's got the waxy black braid running from the Land of the Rising Sun to the Kingdom of the Full Moon, for one thing, and no one dresses like that on purpose but the Chinese.*

Li must have come in on the Paloma [*that's the name of the ship, H:* La Paloma, *if you can believe that. Try to find out what the cargo was, will you], that's the ship docked at Pier 8. What I took for cat was I guess English, but I'm a monkey's uncle if I can understand it from this far away. Wallace seems to be doing all right, though.*

What's Wallace trying to pull here? Maybe this isn't the job? I decide to let Wallace and the Chinese character finish their business before I grab Wallace and get him to talk sense.

They seem to be bargaining over something, I think a bird Li said. [Bird? Rare birds coming in? What bird, H? Are we talking the junk or are we talking the vertical smile?] Money changes hands—Wallace to Li, meaning Li has whatever it is that Wallace is interested in, dope, wildlife, or women. But why give Li money when Li doesn't have anything to give in return? Or are they setting up another meeting?

What's the union angle that Wallace worked up? [Did Wallace give you his tired tale, too, H?]

Wallace tramps it about 10:05PM. It looks like this was Wallace's real business here after all, despite the tale he told me. Doesn't even look around to see where I am and doesn't stop to detail it with me, just hauls himself over the loose cases and puts boots to the boardwalk until all I can hear is echoes. Li waits around long enough to clean a fingernail with a splinter from the crate he was standing next to and then shoves off without a sound in a launch that he had hiding in the shadows of the pier.

What am I doing here? Wallace hired me for muscle, but he just hands over the money and dusts, probably trying to get away before I show. Doesn't even check to see if I showed at all, and it wouldn't have mattered if I didn't, because there's nothing for me to do except what I'm doing. Nothing. Which I could have done at home, free of charge to Wallace.

Obviously, I need a few words with Wallace, about tonight and about the checks, but the guy is as slippery as an oil slick in a bubblebath. I hightail it back to the Embarcadero after I glom the Chinese character get into his boat, but Wallace is the shadow of a ghost, and I'm left just standing there holding my notebook and not much else.

Archer didn't know what had happened at the pier that night, and maybe Wallace didn't know, either. Hammett sure as hell didn't know. Why would Wallace bother to buy muscle if he wasn't going to show it, and why would he run away from it afterward? Who's afraid of his own muscle?

The first thing they teach rookies at the Pinkerton's is know the client. As a dick, the job that pays might be putting paid to the client's mystery, but the dick's mystery is always the sucker with the money. The casework is only next door to the client when the dick has the wrong house. Archer might have rung the wrong bell at the Wallace place, but he could make up for it with Chandler. He assigned Jack Millar to find out whatever he could on Chandler and the long green that he was showing. Whose lawn was Chandler tending?

[11]

Both Archer and Hammett had Wallace pegged wrong. If Archer had gone down to the Bank of America and Italy, he would have discovered that the P. I. detailed there—our man, Dan Wallace—was also the penman passing bad checks over General Norris Sternwood's signature.

Wallace had been in San Francisco for a month or so, working the security detail at the bank and cashing checks to keep his girl, "Miss Wonderley," happy. Carmen Sternwood might scratch like an alley cat, but she was not about to lie down in the alley with them; after a week or two at the flop on Geary, she seems to have told Wallace to put up or shut up. The pair moved to the Hotel St. Francis, a much more upscale kind of joint, the kind of snoot-shop where kitty-cats with their noses glued to the clouds would feel more comfortable. Trouble was, on his salary from the bank, Wallace couldn't afford the St. Francis any more than he could afford a diamond-encrusted litter-box or a solid-gold doughnut.

Wallace had to come up with more dough, a lot more, and the General's checks would last for just so long. He had already run shin-first into a knee-high wall: he couldn't write the checks for much, or else the bank he was cashing them in would have to get in touch with the General's bank, Security First National (the old Farmers and Merchants Bank), the bank they were drawn on; just standard bank procedure, he knew as well as anyone. He had to come up with another scam and quick, or Carmen would jump ship and go home with her head held high and her tail between her legs. She was that kind of kitten.

Wallace caught a bit of tongue: a bird made of gold and with jewels for eyes was coming in on a slow boat from Hong Kong. Trick was, the bird was covered in a kind of lacquer to hide its value, and so you had to know what the bird was about to know what it was worth. It was from Europe, originally—Malta, if you had to be specific—and an old legend among the checkered-tablecloth-and-Chianti bunch at the Bank of America and Italy. Someone with friends at the docks had found out that the bird was due any day, but couldn't say which boat it was coming in on. Every grayhair in the front office wanted in on the action, but none of them wanted to tell the others, for fear that they would get double-crossed.

Wallace, though, had a good line on the bird through a recently-arrived Greek staying at the Hotel St. Francis. The Greek's name was Joel Cairo, a gladhanding dandy with a business card for your right hand and a stiletto for your back. He spread it around that he was in the market for odd little artifacts and mementos, especially those having to do with birds, and especially those coming from the Orient. Cairo wanted everyone to know, if such a thing happened to turn up, he would gladly take a look at it: there was a worthless little statuette that might be arriving soon, for instance, a falcon in profile. Wallace put two and two together and checked it out with some casuals supposed to be working the docks that week. A ship from Hong Kong was due in two days time, *La Paloma*.

Wallace cashed a check, figuring it to be his last: he would drop the money on the bird, crack the coat of lacquer, and sell it to the highest bidder back at the bank. If no one would bite, there was always this Cairo fellow, though not even Wallace was dumb enough to trust the Greek.

Steps one and two accomplished, Wallace found himself saddled with an unwanted silent partner, Archer. When Hammett called to ask him about the bad checks being passed at his bank, Wallace knew that these Johnnies were on to him, or would be soon enough. He had to find out what they knew and how they knew it before they could catch him out, and before this final play netted him the funds to move on to New York or Chicago, with the wonderful Miss Wonderley and three fat pockets.

Wallace went fishing with the bodyguard lure. It was a pretty safe move, he figured, a good reason to get this sticky dick, Hammett, down to the docks and then dump him in the bay. But in the event, he couldn't get Hammett, the one he thought was on to him. And this dick, Archer, didn't even seem to know what the other one had asked about—he hadn't been down to the bank, for one thing, and hadn't mentioned the bank when they got together at the office. Maybe this square peg was in the dark on the whole business. Wallace took pity on the puzzled peeper and threw him back to swim with the sharks. For one more night, anyway.

[12]

As the questions for Hammett in Archer's notebook show, Hammett might not have been in shape to crawl the city streets, but that didn't mean he couldn't do his share—or a share, anyway—of the work. At least, not when he wasn't scraping the fur off of his tongue. Hammett hoofed it down to the Bank of America and Italy the next day, and Wallace's jig was up. Hammett never was one for Irish music.

Wallace hadn't come in that morning—called in sick, according to the log-book at the bank—but the tellers all pointed down the line of carrels to Dixie Monahan, a pug-ugly brunette with a face like a bulldog with a broken nose and, according to her fellow tellers, about as likely to hump your leg. She was not particular about her male companions, any more than she was about keeping their names a secret; Dixie rolled over almost immediately, confirming that

Wallace was the man that Hammett needed to talk to. She had been cashing his checks for several weeks, despite a little discrepancy in the name on the account and the name of the man cashing them. Hammett returned to the office to pass the straight dope straight to his boss, Archer.

Jack Millar's nose for news had produced some solid scent—probably the correct one, General Norris Sternwood—and the scoop rushed into town to give the lead to Hammett and Archer. But he was all the way out in Los Gatos, and it took him a while to get to their office. Before Millar had even pulled out of the station, Hammett was back from the Bank of America and Italy, and Archer Investigations had a customer: Carmen Sternwood.

What nobody knew, not even Wallace, was that Carmen, Hammett's "Miss Wonderley," was after the Maltese falcon, too. She knew the secret, and she was out to double-cross her boyfriend, who she took for an all-day sucker, the kind that loses its flavor overnight. She knew that Wallace had bought Archer's muscle because he told her so and she went to their office to ask the firm to pin the tail on Wallace that night. She pretended that she was her own sister, giving them the expired story that Hammett starts his book off with.

Neither Archer or Hammett would have known Carmen Sternwood from Adam or, for that matter, Eve, but the name "Wonderley" was better than any mole or sore thumb in figuring who they were talking to. Archer played along, telling Miss Wonderley that he would go to the hotel where she thought her sister was staying and try to get a word with her, alone. But he knew there would be no one to get in touch with. No one, that is, that wasn't in the office just then.

Archer and Hammett might have been willing to let out the rope that Carmen would hang herself with just so they could get Wallace out of the way and the falcon back in its cage. Wallace would definitely be on to them if his Miss Wonderley didn't show up for dinner and the police did, and the falcon would flap away again. Also, not closing the net on Carmen and Wallace just then would give Millar some time to come back with a name on Chandler's moneybags.

[13]

Working the shadow on Wallace would be as ticklish as a two-year old in a bathtub full of feather dusters. Archer couldn't be seen by Wallace or Wallace would know the jig was up, even if the music kept playing; a hand out for a bill that wasn't due yet would be the last thing that Wallace would expect if Archer was still in the dark on the falcon. If Archer played the next passage *a due*, Wallace would see that Archer knew the whole tune, and start in with the coda. But Archer still had to be seen by Wonderley/Sternwood, or else she would know the musicians weren't playing at all and demand her nickel back. She had to think she was getting her money's worth and that meant that Archer had to be there at the hotel, both seen and not seen.

Here's the only passage on shadowing in Archer's notebook (as usual, he and Hammett are arguing):

> *H— The shadow isn't a sport and it's not a job either, not exactly. That's where you're wrong. It doesn't matter if you do it every week, like Holy Communion or a game of catch, and it's not in the feet or the shoes, or even in the way you walk.*
>
> *It's all in the head, and if you don't have it to start out with, you're not going to pick it up just by practicing.*
>
> *You have to watch your own shadow. I mean the one that only comes out when it isn't twelve noon.*
>
> *It's there all the time, but you almost never notice it. When it's right in front of you, it looks like nothing. If it's going alongside of you, you might catch it out of the corner of your eye, but if you turn to look at it, it'll turn a little too. Most of the time, it's behind you, but not so's you'd notice. It's slippery, like a railroad accountant on payday.*
>
> *Your shadow's got the jump on you, because it really is walking in your shoes— if you look down, there it is, coming up out of your wingtips, like a pair of pants you just took off and haven't got around to hanging up yet.*
>
> *Beale is a man of habits. Everyone is. You'd go crazy trying to think up something new*

every day. So you go back to the same old, over and over, till you don't notice that it's the same old. But since you're not on the beat for the same old, you have to be on him all the time. Any day, the same old could get old, and disappear, right along with the beat.

The shadow is not just in the beat's shoes, the shadow is in his skin. Just pops out when the beat is least likely to notice. Your shadow gives you as much space as it can—it gets the longest when you're out in the open and the sun is shining, but it always snaps back when you turn a corner or get into a small space. That's what I'm trying to do here, I guess. Snap back, waiting for him to slip up.

[It's just that Beale is onto the game. We gotta get a new set somehow. Maybe try a new op, if you know anyone. Not you. You couldn't keep up with him anyway. Spring it on the dame, H, see if she'll cough up enough dough for another op.]

Even if you could pin a tail on this guy, he would shake it. Beale knows the city like a ballplayer knows his glove. He uses windows on me, doors. Anything he can find. Slippery like a sardine pretending to be an eel.

Normally, you got a guy using windows on you, you use that against him. If you're a clever dick, you set up inside some joint, then he's too busy checking his pearlies and the angle of his tie in the reflection to notice you on the other side of the glass. The beat's own nose is the perfect cover—if he can't see past it, you're in the shade. Beale might glom me every once in a while, sitting over my plate of beans in John's, but he would be looking right through me—his eyes would see me, but his mind wouldn't.

On the street, though, with nothing between us, he makes me like a ham on rye, mustard, no pickle.

The Pinkertons'd have five, six, eight guys working on this, one on the inside, another on the street, and all the rest at places he's likely to turn up, but here it's just me, and I can't quite cover for eight guys. Three, maybe. Four, tops.

I know he'll pass by the newsstand on Mason at a certain time of day, and I can catch him waving his nickel then if I want. But that won't tell me where he's going, so if he shakes me again, I may as well have never spotted him. This mug's got a map tattooed on the inside of his eyelids.

Even with the tail I could never make him for more than four or five blocks. After that, he was dust—just another haircut and pinstripe suit. I never liked the tail anyway—all it tells you is where the beat is headed. You'd be better off figuring out why, not where, because then you could get in front of him, and in front you got the best view.

There's a good reason why we've got a head for mugs—that's where all the features are. And the features are all there, on the front, because nothing's going on in the back. Not even fronts are doing business behind their backs, just behind their fronts, if you get my drift.

It's all up front. Everything's a front.

Maybe you might catch someone putting the bite on a sucker from behind because you can see the crooked deal, but you still wouldn't know the trick because all you would see is the crooked deal. You wouldn't know the rest of the deck; it'd be like playing cards with four Aces of Spades. You would never know it was crooked.

All right, if it's all a front, then maybe fronting's the answer, you say. Yeah, well, maybe, but with the front, you gotta be so quick and so smart that you know even more than the beat you're fronting, and that ain't always practical. Some beats, I'll admit, that's the easiest thing in the world. Polhaus, maybe, or Dundy, but Beale ain't one of them. Beale shakes me when I try to front him.

You have to react quick with the front. You turn before they turn—you might know the guy inside and out, but if you're looking back over your dandruff the whole time, you're going to get caught with your hand in the cookie jar more times than not.

It's easy enough to be seen when you want to be. Easy enough, too, to not be seen, if that's what you're after. But to be both at the same time? It's like someone telling you to act natural, or not think of a pink elephant.

[14]

That night, according to Hammett's truncated account in the files and Archer's somewhat more detailed account in the notebook, Jack Millar, after reporting to Hammett what he had found, was instructed to go down to the St. Francis where Archer was already staked out. Hammett handed him the first thing that came to hand, a well-oiled copy of *Black Mask Magazine*, and told him to hide his face behind it, holding it upside down so that Archer could make him out in the crowd. Between their haircuts, the cut and color of their suits, and their vital statistics—not to mention the fact that, as Hammett put it in the notes from the case, "the backs of their heads were practically separated at birth"—a sucker could get the two, Archer and Millar, mixed up, especially if he or she didn't get a good look at their faces. Someone like Wallace. Or

Wonderley. Millar was warned to be on the lookout.

Archer showed at the St. Francis before Wonderley, to scope out the place—he double-timed it down Sutter to beat Wonderley back to the hotel, with Hammett still blowing last night's bitter dregs over the office blotter at the wonderful Miss Wonderley, aka Sternwood. Archer figured that a suspicious, double-crossing flash like Wallace wouldn't chance stashing his retirement account in a luggage berth at the Pickwick Stage Terminal; where else do you put the dream score but under your pillow? Either the goon was already in his room, or else he was on his way over hill and over dale to the hotel.

While they were waiting for the party to start, Archer asked Millar what he had found on the money behind Chandler. Millar repeated what he told Hammett about Chandler's Los Angeles connections, probably giving Archer the name that he was looking for—Sternwood. Aside from the Lloyds, there weren't any other names that Millar could have given Archer.

Archer laid out the plan: he had to be in two places at once, so he would need Millar to be in one place, playing him, while he, Archer, would be in the other. He told Millar to stay in the lobby until he saw Wonderley pass by; Millar would know her, he said—anyone with hair on his chest and feeling between his legs would know her the instant he laid eyes on her. When Millar was sure that she had made him he was to take the next cable car home and put the whole thing out of his mind. Archer would be set up in the alley behind the hotel, on the off-chance that Wonderley was passing the news to her boyfriend so that he could climb down the fire escape with the falcon. No matter what Wonderley was up to, Archer would be in position to catch Wallace coming out or going into the hotel when he passed by the alley on Geary. If Archer spotted Wallace on his way in, he would signal Millar to hightail it out the back way, in case Wallace caught sight of him and doubled back to drop the hammer on what he thought was Archer. If Millar caught sight of Wallace, he was to pass the word to Archer about which way the flash was headed.

It didn't work out that way though.

Wallace was already up in his room when Archer and Millar arrived at the hotel, holding the falcon and waiting for the phone to ring. When it did—if it did—he scrammed without waiting for his kitty-cat to show her pretty little face. Wonderley walked in the door just as he was walking out, and missed spotting Millar across the lobby, who missed spotting Wallace. Wallace, though, didn't miss a trick. He made Millar with the pulp rag in front of his face, staring over it at him, and fingered him for Archer. He stopped with Wonderley just long enough to smooth her skirt, and then hit the doors. Not seeing her peeper, Wonderley waited a beat or two in the lobby.

Millar, having spotted the dame, split, as per Archer's plan. Wallace had doubled back on Powell though, and by the time Millar walked out of the lobby into Union Square, Wallace was just a couple of steps behind him with Millar none the wiser. Millar was supposed to be catching the intercity back to Los Gatos and Annie, but he must have changed his mind before he made it to the Market stop. He headed west on Geary uptown, maybe hoofing it to the library or City Hall. Or maybe something in a birthday suit and a red light caught his eye. We'll never know.

Wonderley held back a few minutes, but caught Millar through the lobby windows, and, thinking it was Archer, swung out onto the street after him. She was at the door when she spotted Wallace passing by and held off a few beats to let him get a little ways ahead. Archer was in the alley:

> *I'm in a puddle of something dark behind the St. Francis, watching the service door and the fire escape and trying not to get rats on me, when I spot Wallace passing by down on Geary. By the time I shake the plague off my brogues and step out of the shadow of the St. Francis, he's already almost to Mason.*

Wonderley pops around the corner just before I step out of the alley and it's a good job I don't run into her. I let her pass and give her some room to grow on, too, while a guy in a chef's hat yells some pally-voo at me and dumps a pot of something hot and French into the alley. I don't have time for a lesson in Anglo-Saxon, so I give him the appropriate hand sign and jog to catch up.

Lucky I spot Wallace headed up the hill when I hit Mason. I cross in front of the cable car in the middle of the intersection and head north on the opposite side of the street to watch the rest of the parade, Wallace, then Wonderley, nearly a block back and fighting the holiday crowds to keep her peepers on Wallace. Some little fellow in short pants and a wool jacket stops me to ask where his mother went. The kid's got a face redder than most rummies and enough water coming out of his peepers to drown a cat. I give him a pat on the head and a push downhill. Good luck, kid.

On the south side of Sutter, when the slope up to Bush gets to where you'd have to stop and light a cigarette so you could catch your breath and pretend I didn't know you were out of steam, H, I'm finally close enough to see the soles of Wallace's cheap shoes.

That's when I spot Millar, stopped at the newsstand. What's the rumpus? He's *supposed to be on the intercity heading home.*

Wallace pretends to pass him by, but he's giving Millar the eye like a lion watching the lion tamer. I shoot a poison-tipped look at Millar to get his attention, but he's got his head in the paper and his mind somewhere else and I throw foul.

Wallace slows down and stops at the end of the block, ducks into the doorway of the apartment building at the top of the rise. I can't risk him eying me, so I duck into the shallow alley right across from Wonderley, about halfway up to Bush. Some gee behind me gives my neck a sauna with his nose before shoving past me into the street. Must be a real toney customer, living in these digs. I step on his foot as he passes.

Wonderley is pretending to look at a pair of shoes in a shop window about five yards up Mason from Sutter, but she's really watching the entry of the apartment building Wallace is hiding in out of the corner of her eye. She's only as obvious about it as a rattlesnake on a slice of sourdough.

Millar finally drops his nickel in the newsboy's cup and turns out into the crowd on Mason. He's got his head buried in the paper, flipping through it to find something. He lets the crowd carry him up

Mason until he gets to Bush, then he turns back towards Chinatown.

By now, Wonderley has crossed over to my side of Mason and then crossed Bush uphill. I lose her in the crowd. Wallace exits his doorway ahead of Millar, but he's watching over his shoulder. He just catches Millar's turn in time, and turns with him when he gets to the sidewalk on the opposite side of Bush. I follow them up Bush, but I lose sight of Wallace altogether until I see him surface in the middle of a bunch of Santa Clauses whooping it up in a paper bag before their shifts on the Square. He gives them the time of day and some choice seasons' greetings and then re-crosses Bush to the south side. Now he's in front of Millar, just barely, but Millar doesn't seem to see him. Millar is now less than a block behind Wallace and closing fast. He's going to cause a jam up if he's not careful.

When the two get out of the crowds, right across from the mouth of Monroe, Millar is practically tripping over Wallace, not even looking up anymore, just reading his newspaper by the streetlights. Trouble.

Wonderley has gone up the hill and back down Monroe. She pops out and crosses behind Millar just before Burritt and the stairs down to Stockton. I have to duck into the doorway of Levi's to avoid crashing into her, and I feel like the bunk, like an armchair sleuth missing his armchair. I wait four ticks before showing my head, only now I don't see any of them.

On a hunch, I take the steps down to Stockton, but before I can make the last riser, I hear the timpani of a loose hand cannon up the hill behind me, signaling the end of tonight's performance.

The body rolls down from Burritt, so close the splash stains my pants cuff, and I slide back under the tunnel to dodge whoever pulled the trigger.

Millar. Shot in the head, the poor sap. The coroner's going to have a hell of a time. Hope nobody lifts his wallet in the meantime. Whoever they decide he is, there's going to be a closed casket on Sunday.

If Wonderley and Wallace both thought that Millar was me, then the barrel candy had my name on it.

But why not just duck me? Why shoot? The whole thing stinks.

By the time I make it up the grade on the other side of Stockton, Wallace and Wonderley are just memories. I take a peek into Burritt but it's empty and there's bound to be some heat headed this way. I run back down the stairs and take Stockton back to the Square, to stake out the St. Francis.

> *By the time I make the next block, Sutter, I catch Wallace rounding the corner on Powell at the Sir Francis Drake, but before I can smell the cheap on the doorman's cigar, he's gone, either up to a room or out into the city.*
>
> *What gives? Why the long way around? Why not just head up Powell—unless it was to draw me out, pin the lead carnation on my lapel, even if it was Millar that got it instead? Wonderley wanted us to think that she was playing it her way, but maybe she was in the sandbox with Wallace all along.*
>
> *Two questions: Who pulled the trigger?*
>
> *And who's in the Sir Francis Drake?*

That's where the entry ends, but we know the rest of the story because it makes the morning edition. Lewis Miles Archer, deceased. Iva Archer, mourning wife, only surviving relative. There might have been a smaller item a few days later, in the *Los Gatos Mail*, about John Macdonald Millar not returning home on the night in question, but if so, it's gone missing, buried in a section nobody bothered to archive. Might not have been the first time Millar didn't come home.

The notebook doesn't make it into Hammett's hands, because Archer's supposed to be dead, and Hammett isn't in on the joke. They might not have been the closest of friends, but Hammett mourns the loss all the same. Maybe just the loss of his paycheck. Archer Investigations closes its doors a few days later, after the falcon is disposed of.

[15]

The statue of Victory, looking out through Miss Spreckels's marbles over Union Square that night, wasn't the only one watching Millar and Archer, Wonderley and Wallace. The asset-recovery man, Ray Chandler, was in the mix, too, keeping an eye on the peepers who were supposed to be keeping their peepers on the General's little girl.

Chandler fancied himself a clever dick just like the two Pinkertons he had hired. After all, he did a bit of peepery for a living, too, didn't he? He handed Archer Investigations a simple case and expected a simple—simple and quick—answer. When it wasn't forthcoming, he moved to protect his interests. He couldn't be cut out on a favor to the General because he couldn't afford to look like a fool if he hoped to move into Pascal's place at South Basin and into Pascal's bed in Los Angeles.

Chandler was in Union Square that night following up on a tip that his charge might be staying in the St. Francis when he spotted her exiting the hotel in hot pursuit of some shaving mug missing his soap and holding a package. He probably also spotted Archer, but, since he had never seen Archer (Archer was out of the office when Chandler came in with his case, and out of the office running down leads in the intervening day), he had no idea that this was his peeper. And because it was probably Millar and not Archer at all, Chandler might have been right, despite himself.

Chandler tried to pin the tail on daddy's little kitten, but lost her about where Archer seems to have lost her, after the turn onto Bush. Chandler was tailing from too far back, as any dick worth his cardboard would tell you. You can't see past the next intersection with the slope in the way. Being that far back, though, lets you see things that you might have missed up close.

Chandler should have been in position to catch the whole drama on Bush, including the gunplay and the actors involved, if not the director and the orchestra. His lips were buttoned, though, the surgery paid for with the General's do-re-mi. He should have also caught Archer, the real Archer, down below on Stockton, rushing for the cover of the tunnel, even if he didn't know that it was Archer, or why he should care.

The rest of it played out as Hammett says it did. At least, all we have to go on is Hammett's account, and, for what it's worth, the SFPD file on the falcon, so we've got to believe that Hammett is giving us the straight dope, or something close enough to burn like it.

[16]

Hammett's story of the falcon's origins is about as real as his falcon was, but it was the story current at the time, and Hammett had every reason to buy it. According to that story, the falcon was made by the Knights of Malta, a.k.a. the Knights Templar, God's own goon squad, as a present to the King of Spain, Charles V, who gave them the island of Malta in return, although probably he really gave them the island because the Pope was running a religious protection racket, or else the Knights had performed some service that had to be kept under the table, and this bird was their token payment.

A sailor snatched it on its way from Malta to Spain, one of the salts on the boat, and because the bird was pretty under-the-table, too—maybe a religious relic swiped from some sucker (they called them "infidels" and "heathens" back then, but the words mean the same thing)—nothing more was said, at least on the part of the king. But the Knights didn't cotton much to the theft of their precious bird, and kept dogging the sailor from port to port. That's how the story got out, anyway—the Knights flapping their gums at enough people that the loopy tale eventually got around—and pretty much every sailor who'd been through the Mediterranean knew the flap about the falcon.

So far, so good. Wallace/Thursby hears about it from one of the trustees at the Bank of America and Italy, who he's got waiting on the hook at the Sir Francis Drake Hotel. According to Hammett, it's a guy named Gutman, Caspar Gutman, a Brit, who then passes the story on to Hammett. But this doesn't fit with any member of the bank's staff at that time, or with the register at the Sir Francis Drake. This Gutman doesn't show with the police, either. But Hammett has an answer for that—in *The Maltese Falcon*, Gutman splits before the boys in blue get clued in. So maybe there's a Gutman there after all. We couldn't know, one way or the other.

Whoever Wallace is trying to sell the bird to, it doesn't make it to them. It winds up with the SFPD, in an evidence room somewhere, collecting dust, just like it collected layers of black lacquer under the tar-mops of bored salts up to then. Because, again, according to Hammett, the bird is disguised by being painted to look like it's worthless, to cover up the gold that it's really made of.

One little flash of that gold shows in the notebook:

> *The bird makes its way to SF on a Hong Kong steamer, stolen by Li, or by Li's contact, either in transit or before.* G [could be Archer means "Gutman" here, but he just writes "G," so he could just as easily mean any gee at all] *spreads the little tale about the bird, knowing that the bird isn't gold at all, just hollow lead cast in the shape of a falcon, playing off the old story—but how does he get the right bug into the right ear (Wallace)?*

Looks like Archer had a little time alone with the bird. Hammett shows the bird as a fake, too. It's just lead, in the end, painted to hide the fact that it's just lead. The SFPD has it as lead, too, but Archer says it's hollow lead. Maybe it wasn't the first he'd heard of it.

There's at least one likely customer back at Wallace's bank, a man named Théodoro Ares, who dusts and leaves the bank and San Francisco just after the whole falcon mess blows up, the only one at the bank, apart from Wallace, to do so.

But the players and their lines get hard to track after December of 1928 because the case never makes the papers, except for Archer's murder, and that's not tied in with it according to what the papers know. The General hushes the whole thing up, as much as his deep pockets can, and Chandler escorts the girl back down the coast to Los Angeles, where he stays, now in the General's good graces for bringing his pride-and-joy back home before she gets him in real trouble. The General doesn't know about the murder, but maybe, just maybe, Chandler does.

[17]

Which leaves Archer out in the cold, on Union Square in mid-December with no hearth to go home to. Hammett's account of the events after Archer's murder in *The Maltese Falcon* doesn't exactly paint Hammett in the stained glass as the White Knight, so there's probably some truth to it. In the novel, Hammett gets wrapped around Iva Archer's little finger, turns the bird over to the police, and lets Wonderley flap in the breeze.

The girl stays out of the picture—that's sure. Daddy's money takes care of that. Carmen Sternwood heads back down to L.A. with Chandler, smelling just as sweet and innocent as she did when she blew into town, and Chandler uses what he knows as a lockpick to get into the front office at South Basin.

In Hammett's version, the falcon is supposed to be turned over to Gutman before the police, and it turns out to be a fake. Well, of course we know that it *is* a fake—just lead, no gold—but maybe that doesn't matter to the highest bidder, Gutman or not. Archer's note, about the bird being hollow, maybe means that there's something inside of it that gets let out of the cage when it reaches the Sir Francis Drake, and then after that maybe the falcon really is worthless. Worthless because it's empty, not because it's lead.

Gutman or his shadow then flies the coop, along with his muscle, Joel Cairo, who, in Hammett's version, ices Wallace/Thursby before he goes. Fortunately for Wallace, things don't turn out that way. We know from later events that Wallace dusts, returning to Los Angeles and the General's payroll. No word on why the General would take him back.

Nobody gets rung up for the Archer murder. Wallace/Thursby doesn't figure in any of the police reports on the killing, and neither does the girl—if Archer was the only one to put two and two together about the falcon, and he gets iced by the pair, then there's nothing to connect the yegg or the hellcat to the crime, the falcon to the murder. So how does the statue make it to the police at all?

The entry in the SFPD evidence log has Dan Wallace with nine tenths of the law over the bird, the other tenth belonging to some gentleman who doesn't give his name. It's turned over as stolen goods "acquired" on the Black Market. No one's putting in a claim, so there's no reason to charge the goon. But if no one's claiming the loss, why go to the police at all? And why don't the police question Wallace about the Archer murder? The falcon gets entered into the evidence log, but without a case number to go along with it, the instant it hits the shelf, it no longer exists.

Maybe the police don't dig up any eyewitnesses who don't have their hands in General Sternwood's pockets. After all, if Wallace gets fingered, there's a pretty good chance that the police get Carmen, too—at the very least, her name gets in the papers. So that's a no go, for everybody.

The best place for a pigeon that's delivered its last message is a shoebox under the roses. In this case, the Hall of Justice, in a police evidence locker right along with all of the other three-legged stool pigeons, drowned rats, and crushed bugs, where no one with half a brain would ever think to look, and only the half-witted have keys.

Archer himself stays in whatever shoebox he finds shelter in. There's nothing in the notebook after that night for nearly a month, when pen and ink find the dick on the lam in the City of Angles. Or is that Angels?

[18]

There are so many loose ends flapping in the breeze at the end of the falcon case that it's a whole lot easier to leave them flapping than to try to tie them up. Hammett has his go at it, but in the end, it's a lie—that's what makes his book a novel and not a tell-all. Archer isn't dead, "Miss Wonderley" isn't in jail, and Hammett doesn't get the girl.

Iva Archer throws Hammett over, or Hammett gives her the old heave-ho, but not until the ship's weighed anchor. In *The Maltese Falcon*, Hammett paints himself as the rescuing bluejacket, throwing the alabaster doughnut to the drowning damsel. Maybe he wants it to look that way, at that point in time. But at the time of the falcon case, he's just a swinging dick, wondering what in the hell happened to his boss and where his next paycheck is going to come from. He can't go it alone.

Hammett gets a job writing sales copy for a downtown diamond exchange, Albert Samuels Jewelers, and quickly turns into a real rummy. He maybe takes a little look around in the off hours, but drinking is a full time occupation when you've got a day job on top of it. Still, Hammett has to know something's up, because he knows about Millar, and about the man's resemblance to his boss. Besides, Millar's widow, if that really is what she is, would call him up first thing to see if Hammett knew anything about her beloved missing Jack. Ain't been seen lately. Maybe he was Shanghaied? But then again, maybe not. After all, maybe it's not the first time Jack's gone missing. Maybe Iva convinces Hammett with a peek of peach and a sniff of sour milk to stay away from the police and Millar's widow with what he knows, so that she can collect the life insurance on her good-for-nothing husband who has taken the air, dead or just deadbeat.

Then again, maybe Hammett doesn't know anything is up, because he doesn't offer up anything on his boss to anyone at all, just keeps his trap shut and hums along with whatever tune the band is playing. Maybe the guy is as dumb as he plays. Iva Archer cashes in the life insurance policy and lives just fine on it, but she's out of the limelight and deep in the citrus groves. She leaves San Francisco and Dashiell Hammett behind.

Meantime, Archer gets out of San Francisco and down to Los Angeles, where he resumes his notebook and his profession. Under the name "Ted Carmady," he inks a lease on some office space on Hollywood Boulevard, at Western. He hasn't even had time to get a private telephone exchange or a second chair put in before his first customer walks through the door.

[19]

Joe Brody: a sad sack in a sad suit, rumpled hair and rumpled jacket, but shiny new shoes and a brand new black fedora. He might have had style once, writes Archer, but he was trying hard not to show it. Like a pimp on parole.

Brody wanted Carmady in on a missing girl case that he couldn't go to the police with because Brody wasn't entirely a straight gee. There's nothing on Brody in LAPD files, for reasons that will become clear as mud later, but Archer's notes have the man as hailing from the East Coast, new in town. Back east, Brody had been dealing from the bottom of the deck, always showing 21. That is, until little Carmen Brody came into the full blush of young womanhood. Probably not the words that Brody used.

Carmen Brody was the adopted daughter of Joe Brody. So he said. Brody wasn't really her papa, of course—never had been one for official documents. He wasn't the type of guy you'd see down at the courthouse, not without he's in a pair of bracelets. He'd picked the kid up off the streets of Philadelphia, or Paducah. Or Pacoima. Or Pomona. The city's not important.

What is important is that Carmen turned into the kind of kid that might kick up a fuss in any of those places—she had a figure that would cause a stir even in a seminary. If Brody couldn't turn his back on a castrati in a canvas sack, he couldn't expect a chorus of angels out on the streets of Hollywood. Not exactly.

And now Carmen had walked out on him. Maybe it was Waterloo all over again, but he still wanted to fight it. Unfortunately, the lead he had was one that he couldn't follow unless he wanted it turned into a leash: the cops had the place under surveillance. Like Archer thought, not entirely a straight gee.

Brody passed over a picture of his Carmen. It had seen a few birthdays at least, or else it was made to look like it had. In the snap, Carmen looked like she had seen her fair share of birthdays, too, more than Archer would have guessed from Brody's little story, but she definitely had it, he had to admit. The puss he had in front of him could have launched a couple dozen ships, but the pic was designed to sink all swimmers. It was a cheesecake pic, what they would call "tasteful" these days, but plenty cheeky, if you can take the hint, shot from behind, with the dame wearing her birthday suit and looking over her shoulder down at a sash that was all she had in the world. It didn't look like the kind of thing that a proud papa would be carrying in his wallet; it looked like the kind of thing that a pimp keeps in the palm of his left hand, to keep from being bored, and to get you to front him his fee before he sticks you with the ugliest nag in his stable—long nose, bag of oats, and everything. You can take a ride, but the saddle sores last a lot longer than any fun you get on top of the nag.

Brody's pic, he told Archer, was taken by a man down the Boulevard, a man by the name of Steiner, Harold Hardwicke Steiner. Brody wasn't supposed to have it. He wasn't even supposed to know about it. Turned out that Carmen had been modeling for Steiner on the sly, to make a little money to ditch her old man with, to fly the coop just as soon as the cage door swung open. And then it had.

The pair were pretty new in town, put up at the Roosevelt until they could find a little house somewhere, and Carmen was almost never out of Brody's sight. He was retired, and had all the time in the world to keep an eye on the apple of his eye. But she had disappeared one day when he sent her down the block to the diner for some ham and eggs. That must have been when Steiner got hold of her, he said. She had been gone for a week now, and Brody didn't know where she could be. He spotted the picture while he was getting stinko in the piano joint next door to the diner he had sent Carmen to, in some punk's hands who didn't deserve to breathe the same air as his little kitten. Brody corrected that with some harsh words and more than a few greenbacks. That was when he found out about Steiner's shop. Found out what kind of business Steiner really did.

Steiner was a rotten apple with a glass eye and a forehead that went all the way back to his tailbone. He wore a hairpiece that a blind man could spot at twenty paces, and dipped himself in a cologne so nasty it made dogs dizzy. Despite his trade, Steiner wasn't interested in women. That's why he stayed in business, Brody told Archer. They were just pieces of meat to him. Eat them up and move on to the next plate.

Carmen wouldn't be with Steiner—he already had what he wanted—but Steiner would know where she was, so said Brody. He had to have been the squint that arranged for her to spend her nights away from home. In company, if you could take the hint.

[20]

Steiner's business, at least according to the city directory for 1929 and a receipt found in Raymond Chandler's files, was "Rare Books and DeLuxe Editions." Of what, it doesn't say. No mention of a portrait studio or a red lantern on the premises.

Steiner also makes an appearance in the residential listings, at 7244 Laverne Terrace. The address is in the Hollywood Hills, sure, but in person, it's an ugly squat cabin you can barely see from the road, just like all the other ugly squat cabins on Laverne Terrace. Barely clinging to the hill, like fleas on a dog, but just as hard to get rid of, and just as hard to see until you get up close.

Archer decided to skip the interior decorating and make Steiner's shop after his meeting with Brody.

Brody boards a westbound streetcar at Western (probably headed for the Roosevelt) and I wait for the next westbound, jump off at Las Palmas under the sign of the centaur (a bookshop—"Stanley Rose") and cross the Boulevard.

Steiner's front, 6763 Hollywood, is just cheap plaster scrollwork and plate glass. With the sun shining, I can only really see the scrollwork. The windows are reflections of the building across the street.

This side of the Boulevard is a show joint, The Wild Piano, and a diner that's called "Diner." Brody's diner—must be. There might be some of Brody's cops inside, too, but there might be cops inside of every diner on the Boulevard. It's early afternoon, the coffee hour if you're just coming on for the overnight shift.

The better spot for the copshop is the jeweler's next door to Steiner's, a pawn and prybar type of place, with a tout standing outside. They've got enough flash in the window to blind you even at midnight. Natural place for a cop to be.

Steiner's place is shut and stays shut. I wait until five, first in the diner and then just walking out along the Boulevard in with the business crowd, but no one shows and the door never opens. No lights go on inside. No customers go in. No customers come out.

There's no business of any kind. This Steiner must be independently wealthy. The newsie's got his eye out for me, but at least he doesn't try to sell me a shine or one of his sawdust cigars.

Inside Steiner's joint, there are a few full bookcases and an old mahogany desk with a lamp and a ledger on it. Nothing else, maybe aside from some dust bunnies. Steiner's building goes all the way back to a short alley about halfway up Highland before you get to Yucca, but the shop looks like it only goes to about halfway down the building from what I can see from the windows here.

The alley from Highland makes a right turn to squeeze between Steiner's and the jeweler's out on the Boulevard, and there's a door on the side of the building in the alley—locked, with the window blacked—a little ways past where the shop stops. The stack of packing crates next to the door makes it so you can't see the door from Hollywood. Behind them, there's a gray rubber mat turning the color of tanned skin from so much use. That, and a couple dozen baby mice dumb enough to be out while the sun's still in the sky but smart enough to stay in the shadows until the pink washes out and everything goes gray.

> *If you keep going back, there's a padlocked gate at the end of the alley, and on the other side of the gate, a narrow driveway running between a house and a bungalow court back on Yucca.*

The next morning, Brody is back in Archer's office, wanting to know if his new peeper has made any progress. Archer tells him what little he's dug up on Steiner: address and telephone exchange, business license and the fact that the bookstore is doing about as much business as a refrigerator salesman at the North Pole. It's all in the report that Archer pushes over his new blotter to his new client.

Brody tells Archer that Steiner's is a front for a back-room operation, which explains the shallow storefront and the alley door. The back room is a storehouse and lending library, the kind with a subscription fee just to enter. It's an exclusive joint: the trench coat and brown wrapper crowd, the kind of guys who are too scared to talk to anything with a pulse and a pretty smile. Tell your friends, provided your friends aren't the wrong type; the wrong type being anyone who wears only blue in a professional capacity, maybe. Maybe not, though.

Archer's got no other business yet, and no other lead to follow up on, so he keeps up the stakeout on Steiner's. He sets up at the diner, at the Crown stationer's next door to The Wild Piano, out on the Boulevard, as a customer in the jeweler's: anywhere where he can keep an eye on Steiner's front door. But for a solid week, no one goes in, no one comes out, and the lights never come on inside. Boring as any stakeout usually is, and even an old pro like Archer gets a little cracked from watching the curtain and waiting for the hero's entrance.

> *For days now I haven't seen anything in the window but my reflection. Nothing so much as a light on in back or a book out of place.*
>
> *I've got my routine down pat and so does every other Joe that works this block of the Boulevard, from the scabby newshawk on the opposite corner who spits when he has to give change to the stumblebum that sits on the pavement outside of the Piano with a cup that he uses for coins and booze, sometimes at the same time. I walk past Steiner's front door every hour or so, checking the lock, trying to act like a customer who's been waiting for five days for the shop to open. Hell, I don't even really have to act anymore: I have been waiting five days for the shop to open, it isn't all that hard to look like it. But nobody takes the bait, police or pimp. I wonder why, if the shop's being watched, no one jumps me.*
>
> *I've got this little game I like to play, just to give me something to do, keep my eyes sharp.*

I work the angles on the glass of the storefront, trying to catch my reflection in the glass before it catches me. I mean, before its eyes catch mine. When I get even with the alley, I start watching in the glass, just using the corners of my eyes to see when my reflection appears. I think, maybe if I'm moving at just the right angle to the window, I'll be able to see it before I get even with it. It'll be ahead of me. It won't be able to see me.

Mostly, it's a sucker's bet, though. My reflection is always a couple of steps behind me, so I'm even with the window before it shows.

But today, two steps before I would have come up even with the glass, there it is. It's only when I notice that the suit isn't right—pinstripes, not solid—that I realize it isn't me at all. Turns out to be some gee passing on the outside of me.

Funny, I hadn't heard him coming up behind. I make the mistake because I'm expecting my reflection in the window, and for a minute, I see it, even though it isn't me; it's the suit that throws me off.

The gee's looking right at me, but in the reflection. My eyes meet his in the glass and he jumps like he just got pricked by the needle in the haystack. I stop for a minute and his reflection moves out from in front of mine. He watches it all the way down the glass, and then turns north on Highland. For some reason, I feel like maybe I should follow him, but I keep up the stakeout instead.

[21]

After leaving his wheel of cheddar in the vault of the Bank of San Francisco next to his life insurance policy and his good name, Archer didn't have the crumbs to bring in office help at his new set-up in Los Angeles. Instead, he had an outer office door that he kept unlocked during business hours, and a smaller, inner office that didn't have anything worth stealing if some dumb yegg jimmied the button-lock—just yesterday's papers, a few cigarette butts, and whatever the fumigator hadn't gotten around to before Archer moved in. Anyone could let himself in. Anyone, that is, that wanted to see Archer bad enough and would wait around if he wasn't there, or anyone with nothing better to do than kill his morning in a dirty windowless cubicle painted the color of a suite at the Old Graybar Hotel. Like maybe a mug in a shiny black suit turning shinier by the hour, wearing his new hat on his knee, and nearly asleep in the chair. A mug like Joe Brody.

Every morning that week, fresh as the new day in the dead of winter, Brody was already nodding off in the sprung mission chair against the wall of the outer office when Archer turned the knob. And every morning, Brody would stand up, shake off last night's bathtub balm, gladhand Archer into the inner office, and start in on his beef. It was getting desperate, Mr. Carmady, he would say. He had known Carmen since she was a girl, Mr. Carmady, he would say. He had taken care of her. He had given her a new name and a new home, Mr. Carmady, here, in Los Angeles. He had given her time and money, just what she said she wanted, Mr. Carmady. But still she stepped out on him, he would say.

> *"She was a real pearl, you know? Here I am, opening up that oyster, not expecting anything but saltwater and dirt, and instead there's this pearl there. Most beautiful thing you've ever seen, Mr. Carmady. And that one-eyed sonofabtich's snatched her up and put her in a window somewhere. You gotta do something. You gotta poke that Steiner, Mr. Carmady. But good."*

The same thing, every day. When Brody finished his speech, Archer would deliver his lines: if Steiner had the girl or knew whose pillow she was laying her curls on, he would find out, sure, but he had to be free to look at other angles, follow the case his own way. Brody ought to look at other angles, too. Maybe Steiner had nothing to do with it. Maybe the girl wouldn't come back even if Archer could find her. Maybe Brody might be better off just forgetting her.

Brody didn't like that. Hell, Archer didn't think that he would, but he was starting to get a bad feeling about the whole thing. It was beginning to smell like a set-up, like a four-bit sucker trap.

> *Brody is so set on Steiner as the snatcher that I'm beginning to be not so sure. Brody's a sucker, for Carmen at least, and a sucker's right just twice a day. Or is that a broken clock?*
>
> *Not much difference here, from what I can tell. Brody's here first thing in the morning, every morning. The goon's so insistent that I'm thinking maybe there's another reason that he picked Steiner particularly. Like maybe he figures to get something on Steiner outside of business hours.*
>
> *How do I know that this Carmen's really real, anyway? All I got is a picture of a pretty smile and a story as empty as Bronson Cave. I'm stuck on the outside of this business; I'll never get anything but an empty wallet and an empty stomach staring at an empty window all day.*

I'll make Steiner's house, tonight. Then I'll tell this poor sap that the kid's not there, and that he's wasting his money and my time. Get back to detective work for a change.

And like every other day, after the morning's scene, Brody and Archer walked out together into the sunshine and fresh air of the Boulevard the best of business associates, all nectar, ambrosia, and stale cigar smoke. I'll find her, Joe, if she's to be found. If she isn't, I'll find that out, too. Except that this day, according to Archer's notes, Brody didn't part ways at the first westbound car. He didn't even stop to hear Archer's satin-speak. He just started walking, head-down like Charlie Chaplin in a stiff wind, down the Boulevard west, the streetcar clanging up the street behind him, only looking up to sneak a peek back at Archer when he got to the end of the block. Archer stepped out of sight into the doorway out of habit, and waited four ticks until stepping back out onto the sidewalk, jumping off the curb, and catching hold of the passing car.

As Archer passed, Brody was all over-the-shoulder glances and jitterbug games, trying to keep a tail from being pinned on him: he stopped to tie shoelaces that hadn't come untied, bought a paper he didn't need, got his shoes shined, and window-shopped a dress boutique. The fellow had the wall-eye, for sure. But why?

Archer got off the car outside of Musso Frank's just like every other day, but he didn't cross the Boulevard at Las Palmas to take up his usual position in the window of the diner or the stationer's. Instead, he turned north up Las Palmas to Yucca and followed Yucca west to the Hobart Arms, the bungalow court behind Steiner's shop. There was a red-faced chump in blue overalls dragging a stack of packing crates to a panel truck that had jammed its front end into the mouth of the drive, but Archer didn't stop to exchange pleasantries. He climbed the gate and dropped into the alley between Steiner's and the jewelers. Just before he caught Brody's bowed head passing the opening to the alleyway on the Boulevard, he noticed that the stack of crates next to the alley door had disappeared. The panel truck started up and then the glass of Steiner's storefront went all to pieces.

[22]

According to his notes, Archer rushed to make the circuit back to Steiner's shop, slipping back over the fence and dodging the truck, down to Highland, and finally back to the Boulevard, where he crossed over to the south side. He was just in time to catch Brody finish dismantling the last of Steiner's shelves. Brody overturned the desk in the middle of the room and walked back out with as much clang as he had made going in, making another hole where the other pane of glass had hung. When he stepped out onto the street, he was covered head-to-toe in glittering glass and shining like a Christmas tree on fire. People stopped and pointed, but no one made a move to hold him up. Throughout the whole rumpus, the Boulevard was as quiet as a Catholic in a churchyard, like a backlot while the camera is rolling.

An eastbound came between Archer and Brody, and when it had passed, Brody was on his way down the Boulevard west, with Archer across the street and now almost two blocks back. Lucky for him, Brody crossed at Orange and waved off a bellboy with a shoulder brush at the door of the Roosevelt. Archer stopped at the newsstand on the corner to catch up on the Northcotts while he waited for the boys in blue to show.

Filling up Los Angeles County's ears that month was the Northcott murder case, red and black and white all over. Gordon Stewart Northcott and his mother, Sarah Louise Northcott, snatched Sanford Northcott, the thirteen-year-old son of Stewart's sister back in Canada, and together, the family put at least four unfortunates, and maybe as many as twelve, under glass. The boy got the full Roman treatment from his Uncle Stewart—and possibly also his grandmother Sarah—before they put a knife in his hand and told him it was time to take over the family business. He was made a ward of the state later that month, while the D. A.'s office sorted out whether he would be charged with second-degree murder or deported and released to his mother back in Regina. There had been no word from the father. District Attorney Buron Fitts, catching a little steam from the *Times* and the *Express*, let the boy go. Stewart got the rope up in San Quentin just before Halloween the following year, and his mother served her time and went back to the ranch.

Archer shelved the sensational copy when he noticed the panel truck from Steiner's parked on Orange. The Johnnies were still absent.

> *Same truck, all right. By the time I get to the rear entrance, blue boy's panting his way up the ramp with a couple of the crates from Steiner's back room. I go around front of him and give him a load off.*
>
> *When we drop them in the elevator, the car's already full of their cousins. Mr. Big pulls the lever, and up we go.*
>
> *"Thanks for the help mister—I got a bad back. Wife says I ought to quit this racket, but what else I got, you know?"*
>
> *"Can't live with them, can't live without them."*
>
> *"That's the truth . . . say, don't I know you from somewhere?"*
>
> *"Nah. I got one of those faces. Kind you see on everybody these days."*
>
> *"Yeah, maybe."*
>
> *The service elevator is behind a thick door at the opposite end of the corridor from the guest elevator. The gee in overalls drops a crate against the gate to keep it propped and squeezes back in beside me to grab another one. That's when he makes me.*
>
> *"You were behind the shop just now."*

"Couldn't have been me, Mac. I been here all day." I pick up a crate, square in front of my mug, and follow him down the hallway.

"Oh yeah? Must have been your twin, then. Same suit and everything. You two always dress alike?"

"Who?"

"You and your reflection. I seen you jumping that fence over on Yucca just now. Hold it, Mac. Just here."

He sets the crate down at number 413, gives the door a couple of raps, and is already walking back to the elevator when I drop my crate at the door.

"Don't worry, Mac. I ain't a squawker. I don't like this business anyway—you know what's in those crates, apart from lead and cement? Titty books, hundreds of them. Library worth. Cracked a crate on the way over, but don't tell no one. Meant for a . . . uh . . . Mr. Brody. That you, mister? You Brody?"

"Brody? Never heard of him. The name's Marty. Hell, I'm not even from here. My wife and kids and I are here on vacation, right upstairs. Just got in from the Windy City this morning. Geez, they'll be expecting me. Listen, good luck with the back, pal. And with the wife. Plenty of rest and a good stiff drink always helps me."

"Thanks, Capone. And don't worry—I never forget a favor."

I wait in the lobby until the truck pulls away, and then head up to Brody's suite, 413. The crates are vamoose and the hallway's Mojave. I pull up a glass and see what I can get through the door.

"Yessir, I'll . . . I'll drop it . . . I said I'll drop it . . . drop it, if you want me to . . . But she, she's my wife. MY WIFE, goddamnit . . . I, I apologize. I know, sir, believe me I do know. Never should have done it. I realize that. Yessir . . . yessir. Yes . . . I'm sorry. Alright. Alright. Alright."

What's this about a wife? Brody never mentioned a wife. This guy hasn't been dealing from the top of the deck with me.

I decide to press him and knock loud enough to wake the neighbor, who stops drinking long enough to open his door and peep at me through the opening. The bull moose in a bathrobe breathes at me for a while and then mumbles something obscene. He would slam his door in my face, but I'm not standing in front of it, so instead he just walks away and leaves it open on the chain. In a minute, I hear him sawing logs like the first frost just came on and his woodpile is empty.

Brody doesn't make a peep, and doesn't open the door. I stare at the paneling long enough to be able to pick it out of a lineup and then head back down to the lobby.

I inquire about the occupant of suite 413, and the boy at the desk gives me a look like I just asked him where to go to get a room in this joint. He asks me if I'm pulling his leg. I tell him I can't reach that far and he lets me in on the secret: he thought that I was Brody.

Twins, he says. Brothers? Cousins. By the time I've run him out of the family tree, he tells me that he hasn't seen Mr. Brody since he checked in a week ago. Without a wife or a daughter. Maybe he didn't get a good look at this Brody, he says, another fellow checked him in, but damned if the two of us don't look alike. Given the inches and pounds I have on Brody, not to mention the years he has on me, I take this as an insult, but the boy's description doesn't match up with the gee upstairs. I let it pass for now.

The newsboy makes me, too, this time for fair, and puts the copy of the Express *I was scanning into my mitt.*

"This ain't a lending library, Mister. I can't sell a page's got smudges all over it."

I put two bits in the kid's cup and ask him about the fellow with the broken glass on his suit who passed by a few minutes ago.

It takes more than two bits, but eventually his memory jumps up and bites him, and he tells me that the John doesn't come around much, usually just first thing in the morning and then about two hours later, little before ten in the morning. Never at night.

I look up at the Roosevelt and count over from the lobby, then up four floors. I point up to the darkened window and ask if the light up there's ever on. The kid says he can't be bothered checking the lights, not even at Christmastime.

I tell him not to strain himself keeping his hand out like that, and go into my almost-empty pocket for another wagon wheel.

He tells me that that light isn't on at night, but now I mention it, he has noticed it on after the glass Joe passes by in the morning. Usually not for long, maybe a few minutes at most. He never sees the fellow leave, but the light goes out and stays out.

"That Joe ain't alright, mister. Something about him. Listen, mister, you want my advice . . ."

I turn out my pockets and tell him that, at the going rate, I can't afford his advice. I fold the paper and make for Steiner's.

[23]

rcher's notes from the scene:

Steiner's got the stars and stripes in glass on his floor. And then there are the books, pages of books, things that used to be books. There are more pages than there ever were customers to read them—looks like the first week of fall came early in this neck of the woods.

Two round, cleared spaces where Brody stepped in and stepped out. Otherwise, it's glass and books, sea to shining sea.

The desk is about where it was before, but like a working girl in a stable on the Barbary Coast, it's on its back instead of its legs. The bookshelves are not so lucky—one of them is split in half where it fell on top of another, and the rest are starting to go slantwise.

Brody didn't miss a trick. The chairs in the corner and the potted plant are wrong side up; it looks like he even tried to tear up the carpeting in the corner nearest the alley door. Would have been an improvement.

But no spectators, even at twelve noon on a clear day. Normally, a scene like this, you wouldn't be able to clap a peeper on the place for the bumpkins elbowing each other to get an eyeful. No matter how many movie stars walk their dogs down the Boulevard or take the streetcars to work, Hollywood is still a town of hayseeds and hicks, born gawkers to a man.

Whatever else he is, Brody is right: the police have this place locked down.

Archer wanted to know what else Brody was. One thing he wasn't was in jail, where he should have been after what he did to Steiner's. That meant that the story that Brody came to him with was a half-truth, at best. Probably a much smaller fraction, if the fake check-in and the wife were taken into account.

If Brody was really afraid that the place was being sat on by the Johnnies, and he came to Archer because he couldn't be seen by them, then he was either crazier than a one-legged girl at a chorus-line audition, or the police were giving him one hell of a long rope to hang himself with. And if the police weren't on the place before, they sure as hell would be now that it looked like the Somme in 1916. But instead here it was, all quiet on the Western front.

Maybe Brody had been spreading some simoleons around. It is done. But, given the state of his suit, that thread didn't exactly wash with Archer. For one thing, a mug with moolah could get his duds cleaned and pressed once in a week, or at least once in a month; by that last visit, Brody was starting to smell like an egg left out in the sun too long, and you could almost read by the shine on the elbows of his black suit.

No matter how dirty his client's suit or reputation, though, Archer still had a job to do, and he intended to do it.

[24]

Archer rolled up the hill to the number after Steiner's cabin and parked across the street. It was just after sunset: all across America, nosy neighbors were finished watering their lawns and starting in on themselves, getting the goods on the Joneses. Fortunately for Archer, this was Laverne Terrace, and even the nosiest of neighbors wouldn't have noticed a parked car or even a paddlewheel steamer unless they were standing on top of it.

Laverne Terrace was the kind of street that wouldn't have been able to find a block party with a compass and a map. Ten-foot hedges protected stunted trees and scrub lawns from the prying eyes of passing motorists, and sidewalks were something you only saw in the movies. The houses were stuck to the side of the canyon like moths on the side of a lighted tent; twenty steep steps up to the road, and a narrow, winding driveway down to the garage. You might as well not have had any neighbors at all, for all the privacy you got. The only house you could see was the one across the canyon, and then, only if you had a pair of binoculars and a reason to look.

Harold Hardwicke Steiner's shack, 7244 Laverne Terrace, was one plywood partition away from being a bedsheet and a tree branch: the only thing thicker than a business card in the whole house was the ugly paneled door facing the hedge. If there had been a fire in the fireplace, wrote Archer, you could have stood outside and read by the light. But when he got there, the joint was darker than the inside of a bank vault at midnight. The trip up would have been yet another bust, if not for the fact that the front door was standing open.

> *Never a good sign. Like when the gee down the bar smiles at you and he's missing his front teeth. Usually means something bad's coming. Either Steiner or his guest was raised in a barn. Me, I was raised in a stable. I shut the door.*
>
> *I listen for a while, and when the sound of the blood inside my ears stops frightening me, I turn on the torch in my hand.*
>
> *I don't catch anything moving with the beam, so I start hunting for a wall switch. When I turn up trumps and the light goes on, I wish to God I had stayed instead.*

In the middle of the room, there's a body lying face down on the imitation-Persian, making one hell of a big mess. Directly across from the body, at the edge of the thick, black jelly that used to keep the stiff upright, is a throne, and level with it and hovering above the body, a totem-pole on an unpainted secretary, with the panel below the big bird face opened and film spooling out of it.

Judging from the glass eye and the missing brain-felt, the stiff is Steiner. As for who plugged him, the evidence was probably on the film that I've just ruined. Like I said, I wish I had never found that switch.

In the map Archer drew in the notebook, the first floor is one big square living room with a pair of bay windows facing the canyon and a steep staircase along the left wall.

Underneath the staircase, there's a toilet in a cupboard, with just room enough to turn around unless the door's closed, and around the corner from it, a kitchen. There's a back door off the kitchen, and across from the back door, a short hallway to the garage.

In the garage wall of the living room at about eye-level on the stiff, there's a bullet-hole, the work of a .38, and there are a couple of casings near the throne.

Nine times out of ten, where murder is involved, the people who aren't there are usually the people you really want to see. The people who are there are the people you don't want to see. Definitely the case here: Steiner's even uglier than Brody said he was. Then again, he's not exactly in the pink at the moment. If Brody's right, he never was. Whatever he was in life, in death, he's in the red.

The living room is done up like a movie producer's idea of a Turkish harem. The harem of a sheikh that likes the color red. Steiner's on the rug, not in that getting warm by the fireplace kind of way, but in a face-down, spreading pool of blood kind of way.

I check upstairs, to make sure the harem's empty.

The upstairs bedroom is even worse than the living room—it smells like mothballs and liquor, and it's satin or silk down to the pair of slippers peeking out from under the bed. Even the ceiling's covered in the stuff. Like being inside of a coffin, only it smells worse. At least there aren't any stiffs up here.

Downstairs, the garage is empty, too, except for a chalkboard and a couple of chests, full of more silk and a few books. Lucian. De Sade. Petronius. Story time for pederasts. There's a book the size of a small suitcase at the bottom of one, with gold leaf letters on the front spelling out something like Ornithopteria, or some other disease no one's heard of; I'm not a doctor, and my Greek's as bad as my Swahili.

The back door lets onto a small platform built above the slope, with a long wooden staircase leading down into the canyon. At the bottom, there'll be a dirt road, or maybe just a canyon floor that's been picked clean, in case the fire department gets called up. I flash my torch down at the bottom just to make sure nothing's there, and see a couple of broken steps near the bottom, and a rail that looks like it needs repair. That, and a pair of tire tracks shining back at me, filled up in the night shower.

Back inside, I wind the film back into the camera and put it in my pocket, just in case there's something near the start of the roll that didn't get exposed. I switch off the light in the living room, turn off my torch, and walk up the drive with my collar up. No one makes me.

Everything's Jake at Laverne Terrace, so long as Jake is mum. Police logs from that night don't go as far as 7244 Laverne Terrace, and none of the stiffs match up with Steiner. Archer was probably looking after his client, feeling Brody out before going to the police with the shooting. After all, dead bodies don't clean up after themselves, and they hardly ever leave the house. It could wait.

It just so happened that Steiner was the exception to the rule.

[25]

The next day, and the day after that, Monday, February 4, Brody didn't show at Archer's office. Not first thing in the morning. Not at all. Which was already as queer as the change from a three-dollar bill, even without all of the action of the weekend. When Archer finally gave up on the dope showing—about ten o'clock the morning of the fourth, according to his notebook—he took the streetcar down to the Roosevelt, bill in hand. The Lindy hop might win you a prize at the Cocoanut Grove, but doing the double-shuffle on bad debts and used bullets was strictly from hunger.

On the way to the hotel, Archer stood on the right side of the car to catch Steiner's shop from the window. Somebody had boarded the place up, and there were painters working on the sign on the door and a couple of mountains in dungarees taking out the trash. Pretty quick eviction for a stiff who hadn't started stinking yet.

At the Roosevelt, Archer took a chance and asked the geezer at the desk for his key, the key to suite 413.

> "Mr. Brody? Thought maybe you'd checked out on us. Haven't seen you in a couple of days."
>
> "Paid up, aren't I?"
>
> "Yessir, until the end of next week. Thinking about staying on longer?"
>
> "Depends on how business goes. You know how it is."
>
> "Yessir. Here's that key, Mr. Brody. Have a good morning."
>
> "Thanks."
>
> *Upstairs, the room is as neat as a rye with no rocks. The bed isn't turned down, there are no suitcases on the stretcher, and not a red cent or a scrap of paper on the dresser. No crates from Steiner's, either. There's a towel out of place at the washstand, and a black suit hanging in the closet, but apart from that, it's Bodie after the bust. A ghost town without so much as a single ghost.*
>
> *The black suit is Brody's, for certain. Still needs cleaning. There's nothing in the pockets but stale air. The towel I leave alone.*

Looks like Brody took his crates and dusted. Or else he was never here to begin with.

I pocket the key and take the service elevator down to the freight entrance, to slip the bellboy and the newshawk outside.

I take Selma to Highland, then back to the Boulevard and Steiner's. The sign painters have already finished. "A.G. Geiger, Rare Books and DeLuxe Editions." All they had to change was the name. The mountains are nowhere to be found. Must be lunchtime. I don't even have a window to look at, so I head back to the office.

When he got there, he had a new client.

[26]

Larry Batzel, a sharp from Illinois with a crease in his pants where his brains ought to have been and windsong breezing between his ears, had been dealing faro at a place called "The Cypress Club," down in Santa Monica. He said he was from Illinois, but the old boy sure had a Limey accent; he sounded like a blueblood on holiday as a hooch-hocker. Archer had him down as an ex-British Army regular who had spent time in the trenches with Al Capone's dyslexic brother, or else maybe an accountant taking a correspondence course in English from Bix Biederbecke. Could be both.

Batzel had a job for Archer, a job he couldn't advertise in the wanteds—he was on the lam, see, and he was trying to make a safe house if he could. He had ripped off a gee named Joe Mesarvey, the empty head at the top of the stationery of the Cypress Club, and the real thugs that really ran the place would be coming after him. He needed to blow town for a while, and he wanted Archer to scope out an address up the coast a ways in Santa Teresa. That was all. A bit of surveillance and a one-page report. For this, he would pass Archer a portrait of Grover Cleveland, good at any bank in the land. He had money to burn, and a blaze behind his eyes. What he didn't have was an address or a telephone exchange—he was on the lam, after all. But he was willing to make up for it with a larger-than-usual retainer, if Archer would take him on.

Archer could hardly pass up an opportunity like that, even if it smelled like Fish Harbor at 5 o'clock on August 1st. He took down Batzel's vitals, directions to the sharp farm in Santa Teresa, and opened his wallet to the stolen goods. If the money was dirty, at least the job was clean. Besides, his stomach was as empty as the hole in a doughnut, and so was his wallet.

Batzel would meet him at 8 o'clock, Wednesday, at the diner in the Christie. He intended to make the morning ferry on Thursday if it all checked out. A pretty small window for Archer to get up to Santa Teresa and check out the ranch, but with Batzel on borrowed time and Brody in the breeze, Archer figured that he might just be able to climb through.

Aside from the tinsel in the man's toupee, Archer wrote, Batzel could have passed for old Jack Millar's brother.

The difference is obvious, though—Millar had half a clue and a lot of get-up-and-go, and this Batzel looks like it already went, and it's sliding down his face like a shadow just after noon.

Meanwhile, I got a C-note burning a hole in my pocket and a freight train rolling through the hole in my stomach. I figure to watch the comings and goings at Steiner's out of the diner window.

The ferry schedule in the Express *that newshawk passed me says I'm too late for today's run. Too late, too, to catch the circus over at Steiner's. Whoever this Geiger fellow is, he must be as rich as Solomon or in as tight as Tweed for a rush job like that—the windows are already back up and the place is as clean as Brody's room in the Roosevelt, minus the smelly suit.*

Just as I tip my second cup of Java, in walk the two haystacks from Geiger's clean-up crew, only now they're all cleaned-up. Two blue pinstripe suits and fresh polish on their wingtips. They look like a million bucks: it would take at least that just for the fabric.

They knock a waitress to the floor and send a pot of hot coffee to the same postal code before they're even properly inside of the joint. Then they try to sit on each other's laps while they're still standing up, and upend a table down the row. The Joe in the paper hat behind the counter asks them to leave, without putting a question mark on it.

They pass the booth I'm in on the other side of the glass, about five inches from my face, giving me the wall eye and trying to look casual and doing about as well as a black-tie-only event on fire.

It's not until I finish with my coffee that I see them again, in the reflection on the chrome of the next booth, waiting down the block a ways in front of the Egyptian. Some mugs are so ugly the blur of the chrome is a blessing. There's the usual crowd of nobodies waiting for somebody and, above them like a stand of oaks in a cornfield, Tweedledee and Tweedledum, looking like they're waiting for Alice to show.

With the ferry dearly departed and Brody through the looking glass, I've got time to take the roll of film in my pocket down the Boulevard to Spanner.

I detour around the dolled-up sea-lions outside the Egyptian in the gutter. The two Pillars of Hercules just keep buffing each other's shoes with their peepers, but I know they've got their eyes' hands in my pockets after I pass them. I steal my own look behind when I'm crossing Las Palmas, and, sure enough, there they are, like Mohamet's mountains, on this side of the yokels and making for me.

The expression on the clerk's face when I reach the counter tells me that I've got company on the sidewalk but when I'm back on the Boulevard again with the claim ticket in my pocket, the two goons are in another zip code. I hoof it back up to the diner, just to make sure the twins weren't on their way to Warner-Pacific for a casting call for shaved apes. They must have been waiting around the corner on Cherokee, because they're right back in my rearview when I check it in the window of the hat shop, Mallory's.

What gives?

The eastbound rolls to a stop at the corner, and I wait until it starts up again before I jump on it. The best the two goons can do is to give me the evil eye as I pass. Their heap, that old gray Ford coupe again, is blocked in by a crowd that looks like a Grange hall in Iowa City exploded.

I celebrate giving the monkeys the banana peel by cracking the bottle of bonded in my filing cabinet. May as well catch up on the paperwork while I'm here.

When the bottom of my glass looks like one of Colleen Moore's marbles, I take a peep out the window and what do I see but a gray Ford coupe with two sideshow escapees crammed into its front seat.

The two movers in the gray Ford coupe might have been monkeys, but Archer was the one with the tail. Bad news for an operator—customers don't hire private eyes when they can't be sure about the private part. These two were poison, unless he could shake them. But if they knew where he hung his hat, how could he step out on them?

[27]

After another three-finger salute to the glass on his desk, Archer had a brainstorm. The rain: so far, the two dummies downstairs in the coupe were exercising their eyes plenty but saving their legs, waiting for hide or hair on the street. They weren't after a scalp, just a tail. Maybe he could give them the razz instead.

The thunder: so long as he didn't show on the street, they wouldn't come upstairs to check on what he was doing, just assume that he was keeping office hours. He could backdoor them pretty easy. But if he dodged them by taking the fire escape on Western, they'd still be sitting on his office. Bunk.

The lightning: if he brought them somewhere else, say, the Roosevelt, then slipped down the service elevator and took Selma or Sunset for a couple of blocks to keep out of sight, maybe he could lose them. He still had Brody's key—he could maybe pull the shade, turn on the light, so they'd think that he was laying his head there for a while. They'd sit on the empty room and he'd be in the clear.

He caught the next car, standing near the back to keep tabs on the gray coupe. They were following him all right. He got off at Highland along with half the car—plaid sample cases and Valentinos staying at the Hotel Hollywood—and crossed over to the Roosevelt. He even made sure to tip his hat to the geezer behind the desk before taking the elevator up to 413. The elevator boy was the same character who had been manning the desk Friday.

> *"Say, for a guy who ain't Brody, you sure are around a lot."*
>
> *"Who said I wasn't Brody?"*
>
> *"You did. You said you wasn't Brody."*
>
> *"Why would I do that? I am Brody. I've got his key, don't I?"*
>
> *"Have it your way, Brody. Only don't take the kidding too far. The hotel dick don't like jokes much, and he don't like deadheads either. You just be sure what name you got next time I see you, okay, Mac?"*
>
> *"Pretty spicy talk for a broom-push, kid. You want a tip?"*
>
> *"Sure I do."*

"Don't take any wooden nickels."

"Thanks, mister. You're a real Charlie. Fourth floor."

"Hold it. Here's a buck. Next time, it's 'Mr. Brody,' all right kid?"

"Yessir, Mister Brody. Name's Claude."

"That's one you don't hear every day. Claude, you working the overnight?"

"Yessir."

"There's two fellows, big fellows, bigger than me, even. Clients. Already been chewing the rag with them all day, but you know how it is. It's never enough for these chumps. If they show—you'll know them, they're big as matching refrigerators—if they show, you tell them that I said that I wasn't to be disturbed. Got that? There's a sawbuck in it for you next time I see you, I get a good night's sleep tonight."

"Sure, Mr. Brody. Sure thing."

Before I turned on the lights, I went to the window and placed the coupe. It was parked two cars up on the Boulevard, practically below the window. I turned on the lamp on the desk, made sure the coupe got a good look, and pulled down the shade. Then I put Brody's jacket on the hat tree and dragged it in front of the desk. From the street, all you would see would be a shadow against the shade, about the right height for a gee sitting in the chair at the desk.

Archer was whistling down the Boulevard all by his lonesome before you could say "Jack Robinson."

On the way to his office at Western, Archer spotted a "To Let" placard next to the row of buzzers in the Security Trust Building at Cahuenga. The manager's number is in the notebook: "Klondike 5-1001." If he was going to shake the two clowns singing serenades to Brody's ghost, he would need a new space and a new name. Just then, though, he needed forty winks and a nod.

[28]

Just like in San Francisco, there's not a leaf or a line on Archer's hobbies or home life in any of the old familiar places. Most likely, he spent his nights and weekends in an SRO or boarding house further down the Boulevard, the kind of place where ladies are not allowed in the rooms and the telephone is for outgoing calls only. He was supposed to be lying low anyway, having been murdered in San Francisco. That type of thing can really do a number to your dance card.

Wherever he was laid to rest that night, the following morning Archer was back at the office at Western. Brody wasn't there when he got in, but the gray Ford coupe was. The two pinstripe suits were parked right out front, sporting scowls wider than the coupe's grille, after a long night's watch on the deck of the *Flying Dutchman*. Archer might have lost his shadow in the dark, but with the morning sun, it was back to haunting his daydreams.

With the two nightmares downstairs scaring away customers, Archer was as crossed-up as a teenager at a cotillion. Too many chaperones, not enough dancers. He needed to catch the ferry if he wanted the rest of Batzel's payment, but he couldn't risk the boys downstairs coming along for the ride. Same with checking out the rest of Steiner's cabin. Losing them at the Roosevelt again was probably out: he couldn't blow the same smoke twice and expect his albatross to float on it. He would have to come up with another scam. In the meantime, he couldn't just sit on his hands.

What he could do was to go and see Mesarvey, get the lay of the land and maybe an answer or two down at the beach club. He gave the jilted gees his best come-hither look and jumped in his own jalopy, a 1925 Chrysler not so gently used by the previous owner but in the right price range, according to Archer. It was good enough to get him down to Santa Monica and the Cypress Club.

Santa Monica, at that time, was in the pocket of a man named Marcus Malvern, the sheriff there until 1925. Even into the 1930s, though, Malvern was still the man that everyone answered to.

The city, same as it is now, was a playground for the out-of-towners from Iowa and Kansas and the locals from Iowa and Kansas. Back then, though, they liked their times fast, and their kicks crooked. It was no place for genteel games of tennis at the athletic club and tacking around the bay in your fifty-foot sloop on weekends. There were a couple of boats out in the bay, sure—ugly, ramshackle converted steamers that couldn't make it to Catalina with a tug pulling them—and all of them gambling boats, skirting the law and Malvern's long arms. What was left on land played by Malvern's rules, and didn't dare bite the hand that fed. There were sharks in those waters, just as likely to bite you back; you could wind up with a couple of stumps to show for it.

Malvern lets a place like the Cypress Club hang out its shingle because it's a paying venture, which means that Malvern, and all of his cronies on the police force and at City Hall, collect a bit of the vig and therefore have a vested interest in seeing that the place does better than the gambling houses floating on the bay. But their money stays in their vest pockets; the real winners never get near the slanted tables at the Cypress Club. The money that the dealers pay out, in the unlikely event that they pay out, comes from somewhere else. And that somewhere else is where the big sacks of bills the croupiers rake in get shipped to before they make their way into politicians', playboys', and of course Malvern's, pockets. That is, unless a cannon like Larry Batzel comes along and hijacks it before the take makes it up the food chain.

But a cannon like Larry Batzel doesn't come along very often, because a cannon like Larry Batzel would have his employers, the men behind his employers, and the sheriff's office all after him if he wanders off with a pocketful of their greenbacks. And the sheriff can find out things that the thugs running the club can't, and vice versa. Not even a hole dug to China or a secret cove up the coast would cover up a corpse-in-training who pulled a stupid stunt on the syndicate in Santa Monica. Still, every once in a while, a stupid punk gets a stupid idea that he's a smart punk with a smart idea, and he tries something stupid and half-smart like what Batzel had pulled.

Once Archer and the Ford coupe hit the little beach town that could, the coupe slowed down, and turned off on a side street out of Archer's rearview about three blocks before the beach. At a certain point in every beach town, every street is a dead end street, and Archer was coming to the end. The Ford coupe was racing him there.

[29]

The Cypress Club got its name from the sad wooden specimen leaning against the siding like a drunk not sure if up is still up anymore or if they changed it while he was in the club. The building wasn't that much more impressive. Not judging from the pictures of the joint that have survived, anyway.

Archer slid his jalopy in next to the gray Ford coupe already parked under the shade of the cypress. The two goons holding up the tree's shadow window-shopped him until he got out, then squeezed in through the double doors, ducking their heads as they went in. Archer wrote that it looked like somebody trying to stuff a balloon into a coffee cup.

Archer weaved through the empty gaming tables to the bar where a man who had more hair on his arms than he did on his head stood polishing dirty glasses behind a counter. The two upright elephants watched each other across a door behind the bald baboon. Once Archer had been waiting long enough to get the idea that the glasses were more important than he was, the de-frocked friar with the rag told him that the club wasn't open until eight. Archer said that he was a friend of Harold Steiner's and he wanted a word with the boss. Mesarvey came out to greet Archer himself. The circus watched him as closely as they did Archer.

Mesarvey was a new man in town, running the club for someone higher up and better dressed. He was a snake oil salesman who was missing his snake, with an olive oil complexion that would have to be hosed off by the fire department and a head of hair that belonged on a used Brillo pad. Even his handshake was greasy.

Archer followed Mesarvey into the back room, as clean an office as you were ever likely to find except maybe at the doctor's. Evidently, Mesarvey didn't have much to do to keep the club running. That, or he had one hell of a maid.

> *Mesarvey tells me he's never heard of me. I tell him I've never heard of him, either.*
>
> "You gave my name to Winslow just now, didn't you? Did you just make it up, Mr. Carmady? Or did you know it after all? You do look familiar, but I can't place why."

"What's the difference, Joe? You're nothing but a rubber stamp anyway. An eighth of an ounce of rubber and a whole lot of spilled ink. Who are you working for? And why are your jolly boys there following me?"

"I don't have anyone following you, Mr. Carmady, but I can easily change that, if you insist on being so mysterious. I believe that you said that we had a mutual friend. A Mr. Steiner. Owns a bookshop on the Boulevard. Has a house in the Hills."

"Yeah Joe, that's the swell, all right. Thing is, he ain't too swell these days. Been around to see him lately?"

"No. I'm afraid my work makes it difficult for me to find time for my friends."

"Yeah, it looks like you got enough work here for two, maybe three monkeys with typewriters. But if you're looking to turn out Hamlet, *there are easier ways, Joe."*

"Are you always this witty, Mr. Carmady? Or only when you're trying to impress someone? Why are you here? I am a busy man, you know. This club doesn't run itself."

"Steiner's under glass, Joe. Maybe you punched his ticket."

"Dead? Harold Steiner? Are you absolutely sure?"

"Yeah. I saw the stiff. I haven't gone to the police yet, but I can't hold them off very

long. Not when Steiner's shop gets cleared out in broad daylight, with a detail on it, to boot. Not a very smart play."

"Maybe not, but just what is it that you imagine I had to do with it?"

"It was your men that did it, Joe, the two wrestlers outside."

"Puddler and Yeager? You must be joking. They wouldn't. Steiner is . . was my . . . business partner, I suppose you could say. Puddler and Yeager wouldn't have . . ."

"Maybe you wanted to cut him out of a deal, gave Babe Ruth and Babe Ruth out there a little batting practice with Steiner's bean."

"Not at all. You see, Mr. Steiner hasn't . . . hadn't been appraised of just what it was that he was holding for me. It would have been worthless to him. Invaluable to me, though, provided the right buyer came along."

"Blackmail, Joe?"

He cut that short, slapping his grease-trap down on the table. Probably a buzzer.

"As I've already said, Mr. Carmady, my time is limited. I'm afraid that you'll have to be going."

"One last thing, Joe: any dealers skip out on you recently?"

"In this line of business, there is a certain amount of turnover, yes. Why do you ask?"

"Oh, no reason. If someone was to walk on you, though, would you let them keep on going, or would you turn your little ankle-biters there on them? It seems to me you're better off following the guy with the pig iron than the slug that he's trying to fit into the nickelodeon, if you get my drift."

"I'm afraid that I don't get your drift." He held the last word out like a dead rat that was starting to stink up his sentence.

"I mean lay off me, Joe." There was a shuffling behind me like a pile of leaves falling down a flight of stairs.

"I do have business to attend to, Mr. Carmady. These men will show you out."

The two movers that slid in behind me manhandled me out of the office like a load of waste paper.

All that empty talk in Mesarvey's empty office gave me time to think. If Mesarvey doesn't know what his men are up to nights, that means that they're working for someone else. Someone bigger, with more muscle.

Whoever that is, they started in with the twin big sixes when Steiner's was busted up and Batzel came in out of the cold.

They're not on Batzel, though: they're on me, so maybe Batzel's just coincidence. Or else maybe he's working with them. Unless they're two sides of the same coin, Batzel and Steiner . . .

Which reflection was interrupted, rudely, by being run into a certain cypress tree outside. After I got the stars out of my eyes, I noticed that the bark had peeled off in just the spot that I had rammed it.

Apparently, I wasn't the first to knock on wood at the Cypress.

When Archer shook off the cobwebs, he got back into his heap. A police cruiser flashed its lights at him, and the patrolman leaned out of his window and tapped Archer's Chrysler. Hit the bricks, stumblebum. The Cypress Club was in good with the local law. But was that buy good with the Hollywood hit-squad? How had Steiner met his end?

Before the first turn, the gray Ford coupe was in his rearview.

[30]

With the Colossi of Rhodes in the gray Ford coupe straddling his two jobs, Archer went back to his office. He phoned the manager and took the space in the Security Trust Building, under the name Philip Marlowe. Mr. Marlowe could pick up the keys from the clerk in the lobby whenever he liked. Now all Archer had to do was to figure a way to get rid of the funhouse reflection waiting around every corner, and he would be home-free.

He seems to have gone to Steiner's shop next, where more than just the name had changed. For one thing, there was a real live girl inside, sitting at the formerly empty desk.

The girl could fill out a desk better than any blotter set the Crown's across the Boulevard had on display, and she wasn't doing too bad with her sweater set, either. She gave Archer the name "Agnes Lozelle," when he asked, and informed him that Mr. Geiger wasn't in that day and wouldn't be in later unless he had "specific business." By this she meant that he wouldn't be in to him—not today, not ever. She didn't know anything about the affairs of her employer, and wouldn't be likely to answer questions about them if she did. She just worked there. And he was standing in her light. Archer notes that she bore more than a passing resemblance to his wife, Iva. Maybe she just sounded like a wife. Maybe he was still reeling from the cypress.

Archer tried the Roosevelt next. No one was in Brody's room, but Claude had come on for the night shift by the time that Archer took the elevator back down to the lobby.

> *When the only other sucker in the car gets out on two, Claude pulls the lever and stops between floors.*
>
> *"Listen, Mac, you ain't Brody. I can't see what step you're practicing here, but your dancing partners are some real ugly mugs, you ask me, and they got four left feet. They was in here last night, asking after you, and when I told them that Mr. Brody wasn't to be disturbed, they told me you was Carmady, not Brody. But they were real interested in Brody, though. Real interested. Described some other John to me, one I seen before, but not lately. What do you know, speak of the devil, this John shows last night, and they take off after him like*

stink after a skunk. Bad news all around, mister. You'd do well to leave off with them two. Nearly broke my elevator. We got weight limits; I told them take the service elevator next time. Turns out they don't like jokes."

He showed me his shiner.

"Didn't even really have to try to give me that. Just sort of reached out and touched me. I can't be working looking like this. Know what this does to my tips?"

I gave the boy another wagon wheel and told him to take me back up to the fourth.

Brody hadn't dusted, not altogether. At any rate, he hadn't dusted his room. And Mesarvey's men wanted to be his pal. Brody had had Steiner's stock sent to him—maybe Brody had what Mesarvey was missing. But either Brody lost them or they got what they wanted from him, because they were bright-eyed and bushy-tailed at Archer's office in the morning, not out chasing Brody. And if they got what they wanted from Brody, they wouldn't be bothering about Archer now, would they?

The only thing that hadn't come with the room was Brody's suit. I folded it up and stuffed it down the back of my jacket. Might just come in handy.

Lucky for him, Ted Malvern walked into his office that afternoon, just before he pulled the verticals down over his name. Only a private eye as blind as Malvern could have winked on the ham sandwich chewing the shrubbery downstairs.

With only one more chance to make it up to Santa Teresa to earn the money he'd already spent on the new office space, Archer decided to play the beggar and skip the choosing.

[31]

Ted Malvern was a private eye in name only. He looked like someone had left him out in the sun too long, and, instead of giving him a tan, it had just washed all of the color out of him, like a newspaper left out on a park bench for a week. His father was Marcus Malvern, the sharp in charge of Santa Monica, but Ted was about as sharp as an axe-handle and just about as thick. He had tried to make good on his birthright, joining the force and doing his best to stay out of the way of any real police work. But he found himself playing Esau instead of Jacob when one of Harry Chandler's photographers caught him dead to rights taking a payoff that was due his father. After that, he had no choice but to quit the force and go into business for himself, older and not necessarily wiser.

At that time, in that city, it was a fact of life that you didn't make money as a private eye. Not if you were a straight shooter. Just making a living at the game meant that you had to be plenty crooked. Ted's barrel had gotten so bent that he kept his gun unloaded—odds were, if he pulled the trigger, the bullet would just come back on him.

Ted made his pocket money as a finger man because no one would hire him for any real private eye work, not if they had any kind of sense. The finger man is a professional eye-witness, the kind of guy that is always there and never there, especially when there's something to see or someone to be seen. There in the sense of being convincing to a jury, not there in the sense of, well, not there. Never there. A Pinkerton logo without the nerve to back it up.

Ted identified people the Santa Monica sheriff's office wanted put behind bars, fine upstanding citizens who found themselves on the right side of the law in the wrong town. There wasn't a witness for the defense that Ted couldn't positively identify as last week's bootlegger extraordinaire, cat-and-dog burglar, or midnight flasher of Venice Beach. It was a living.

Not all of Ted's pinches stayed pinched, however. Malvern had put the heavy finger on a half-pint in a ten-cent suit named Carl Lundgren about a month before. Lundgren was a Hollywood high-schooler with a pretty smile and much much more when the money was right. One of the judges in Santa Monica, a bent family man, got caught with his hand in the cookie jar, and Malvern got called in to call Lundgren off. But when the case went too far and the judge pulled some strings. Lundgren was out in a trey. With Lundgren back in the bosom of the law and pulling the judge's string, he was looking for fair play. If Ted didn't want to find his own name on a subpoena, he had his work cut out for him.

Seemed that Lundgren's pal back in Hollywood, Harold Steiner, hadn't been seen in a couple of days. Malvern didn't know Steiner from a hole in the ground, but figured that a Hollywood dick just might. Particularly if that Hollywood dick had already been detailed to Steiner, according to Malvern's father's friends in high places. Friends with hearts as black as the oil that kept them pumping.

Archer could help, all right, but before he could put Steiner back in the hole, the phone rang. It was Brody.

> *"Mr. Carmady! It's . . uh . . it's Joe Brody. Look, I haven't been completely honest with you. Wasn't my choice to make, you know. I'll explain it when you get here. My room's been rifled. They took everything. Room 413, the Roosevelt. Be here in thirty."*
>
> *"Brody . . ."*
>
> *He had already hung up.*

Archer apologized to Malvern—he had to be going, another client, but he had a jimmy for Malvern's jam. He gave the mark the skinny—Laverne Terrace, nine o'clock tonight. But first, Malvern had to do something for him. Call it a retainer.

He brought out Brody's suit.

[32]

Fortunately, Ted was about the right height, about the right frame. The guy was so skinny he looked like an omelet without the eggs, and his face was more minute steak than choice cut, but he would have to do. Archer canned and preserved his objections—it would take him thirty minutes just to get the dope dressed and make the blocks to the Roosevelt, so it was Malvern or nobody.

The cushion from the chair and Archer's extra shirt gave Malvern about the right girth, and after Archer had pulled the hat down to Malvern's eyebrows and the collar of the jacket up to his nose, he could have fooled nine out of ten blind men and maybe, just maybe, two titans in pinstripe suits more interested in the clothes that made the man than the man that wore the clothes.

Malvern was supposed to breeze out the front and cross the Boulevard headed east to the next streetcar stop. If he saw the coupe follow, he was to board the car. If the coupe didn't follow, he was to climb back up to the office. When he got to Vermont, he could flap, leaving the cushion and the jacket on the seat of the car. The goons hunting shadows would see there was nothing behind them, and Malvern could go on about his business, whatever it was, until nine.

Malvern played the puppet without a yank. Maybe he was used to taking orders that didn't make any sense, or maybe he just didn't have the sense to make anything out of them. After he hit the stairs, Archer decided to double his chances and picked up Malvern's get-up. Malvern had looked like a Skid Road urchin in a Salvation Army suit, but when Archer put his duds on, he felt like a Dalmatian in a dollhouse. He packed up his few things while waiting to see if Malvern boomeranged, then started for the Roosevelt. No Ford coupe, no twin titans, no Ted Malvern.

Archer got the key from the drooping clerk at the Security Trust and dropped the few things from Carmady's office on his new desk: his suit, the file on Brody, his spare notebook, and the half-empty bottle of rye. He had to wait for the next car. When it stopped at Highland, he jumped off and hoofed it to Orange. He gave the front entrance the go-by and took the service elevator up to the fourth.

Brody didn't answer his knock. When Archer let himself in, the light was on but no one was home. He left the light burning and sat down on the edge of the bed, well away from the window.

[33]

Archer waited for a while, then he waited for a while longer. On the wall next to the door was a painting that looked like it had been done by a myopic with a migraine.

The de Young, this ain't. I lean forward to see if I can make any sense out of the doodle on the wall, and I feel Malvern's pants giving, like having the family jewels stowed inside of a snare drum. Hope Malvern likes a breeze.

Lucky for me, the split's far enough back that it doesn't show if I keep my legs together like a good little girl.

What I can tell, the painting's of a picket of people on a beach, with some dark rock in the background that goes almost all the way up to the clouds. At least, I think it's supposed to be rock. Not really sure about the clouds either.

I'm just about to give the rock a mustache when the door opens and the Lozelle dame from Geiger's steps into the room.

"Mr. Brody. Please, don't get up on my account."

"You might not like the view. Then again, you might. I'm not a betting man."

"What's that?"

"Never mind. Agnes, wasn't it? The smart dame with none of the answers. Well, Agnes, I know why I'm here, but I can't say I know why you are. This is a married man's room. Or didn't you know that? Maybe you've got an answer to this one: what is a girl like you doing in a nice joint like this?"

"Ah-ah-ah, Joe. The line's 'what's a nice girl like you . . .'"

"I know what the line is, all right. You play nice, maybe I'll get it right. Did you follow me here? Anybody see you come in?"

"Maybe. Maybe you ought to ask yourself who else knows you're here and let me worry about who knows I'm here."

"Sure. That's a good point, sweetheart. Another one I'd like to see the map to. Let's talk it over, why don't we? Have a seat, and we'll play like old friends. Or maybe you're out of practice."

"You want to be nicer to me, Joe. I've got information. Something you want. All you've got is an empty notebook and a lot of fancy talk. And a suit that looks like it's for your nephew."

She tugged a flask with a cut diamond cap out of her cleavage.

"No reason we shouldn't be friends, right, Joe? Neither one of us is getting any younger. How about a drink?"

I could smell gin on her breath. "I only like rye."

"This is rye. Don't you think I know my customers' tastes?"

"I'll call down to the desk, get some glasses sent up."

"Why bother? Are you afraid I might have cooties, Joe?"

"It's not your cooties I'm worried about, sugar. They're probably as cute as you are and just as easy going down. Just that some of the mash lately's been putting pennies on people's eyes."

"Oh, I'll vouch for this stuff. Eddie's a pussycat. He wouldn't steer me wrong. He knows better than that. Bottom's up, loverboy."

I tipped the flask back. All of a sudden, it turned into a bar of greased lead. I remember dropping it onto the bedspread and then the diamond did its work. The cap blurred like the sun through a soaped window and then one of its rays reached out and stabbed me right behind the eye, where headaches go on vacation. Like a bird into a window, I was out cold before I even touched the floor.

I wake up on a boat just about to pull into dock. My legs are wobbly, like an egg that's been in the pan too long, and my head feels like a piece of felt the cat's been at.

The sea's as rough as a porcupine rubbing up against a sheet of sandpaper, and, as far as the eye can see, lime-colored suckers about to make like the Romans after an orgy at the rails. Must be pulling in to port. Some of them I recognize behind the green, but I can't put names to any of the mugs. Not in the state I'm in, anyway.

There's a Lozelle lookalike on the deck below me, wearing a black dress with lipstick the color of a hothouse carnation and holding on to the rail so tight her knuckles go the shade of Tom Sawyer's fence. If it weren't for all that class, I'd say it was Lozelle. Maybe this one's her sister.

Mesarvey's two meathooks, Puddler and Yeager, are here, too. They're not watching me, though. They're facing the other way, towards the skirt. Can't say I blame them.

A bunch of stiffs line up behind me even though I'm not in line. I can't even stand up straight. I manage to stagger down to the front of the gangway, using my fellow passengers like rungs on a ladder, but I run out of shoulders at the front of the line and it's only because they just push me up the plank that I make it to the end of the pier. I drop like a sack of flour left out in the rain, as near to horizontal as I can get right now, which seems to have an awful lot of diagonal in it. Seems to me they made dry land more stable than this. Somebody ought to write a letter to whoever's in charge.

I watch all the suckers file off the boat, but I never see the lady with the lipstick get off. By the time I can stand on my own two feet, the gangplank just drops off into spray and foam. No boat and no lady.

The people ahead of me hoof it down the boards, squeeze between these two big rocks, and disappear, like nickels into a peepshow. Once they're on the other side, it's out of sight, out of mind.

The only things left on the docks are me and some yelling. It takes me a little while to realize that I'm the one doing it. Not a single one of the jerks ahead of me so much as flinches—the slug nickels just keep disappearing into the slit, one after another.

And then there's only Puddler and Yeager between me and the rocks. Now that I'm a little closer, I can see there's a path in the cliff up ahead. I'm halfway to the two lunkheads, still trying to say whatever it is my mouth is trying to say, but they're gone before I can get to them. I can't catch up because I keep making like I'm at a Catholic mass with these rubber legs of mine.

The crack between the two rocks looks just about wide enough for two cockroaches to pass each other, if they wanted to. I keep expecting it to get bigger as I get closer, but somehow it doesn't. I manage to push through at the spot where I saw Puddler and Yeager and the others disappear.

On the other side of it, there's nothing but more black rock, steep as a downtown jeweler's prices at Christmas and just as slick, and a narrow path that I don't manage so much as get managed by until I get to a switchback staircase cut into the wall of the cliff.

Each of the steps is just a little bit narrower than the one before, like the bellows of an accordion wheezing out a B-flat, and I have to turn my feet sideways and scoot up the wall on the last few. It's all I can do to get to the top without pitching out onto the rocks.

The top step is jammed between two buildings that are so tall and so close together that stepping up onto it is like jumping into a photographer's darkroom; it's darker than the bottom of a well at midnight on December 21st. I can't even tell if my eyes are open or not.

I take a few blind steps before I can pick anything out of the dark. Even then, all I get's a cheap mimeograph of the inside of a closet with the door closed. Lucky for me it's level ground and not more stairs.

I look up and there's a big square of light hitting the building on my left, pretty high up. I can't see the sky.

The alley I'm in, if that's what it is, is only a little wider than my chest. That's a good thing, because I can just bump along, even though I can't really see where I'm going. I just keep playing blindman's bluff, stopping every couple steps to see if I can hear the other suckers from the ferry up ahead. But if there's so much as a pin dropping anywhere in this burg, somebody's thought to put a feather mattress underneath it.

Anywhere's as good as anywhere else when you're lost, so I just keep bumbling my way along until the wall on the right ends, and the one on the left keeps on going. I keep on going, too, until I run smack into the wall in front of me. Since I don't have a choice, I turn right.

Down the way, there's a puddle of muddy light as big as one of Steiner's bookshelves and just as crooked. When I get there, though, it's just like everywhere else here—there's nothing there. A wall in front of me, and more black off to each side.

It's either go back to where I've already been or take one of the turns, so I take the right, since it looks like that's where the light's coming in from.

That takes me to another puddle of light and another losing proposition. I take the right again, and then, at the next one, a left, just to be contrary. I keep taking turns for a while, until I can't remember how many I've taken or which way I took them.

It's like a funhouse with the lights turned off. And me the dim bulb. Clear as a glass of milk.

A maze, maybe. The trick to a maze is, you keep your hand on the outside wall and you can't go wrong. But that only works if you know which wall is the outside wall. And if you start the minute you step in.

Me, I'm already in it, and I don't have a clue how to get back to the beginning. If I wanted to start over, I would get just as lost as if I kept on going.

Besides, it doesn't really matter, because it's so dark I can't tell if I'm facing back the way I came in or off to one of the sides. I reach out for the wall that I was following and grab air. Might need a dentist.

I stumble ahead for what seems like three or four miles, and then I see a slit of light off to one side, a different shade of bright than the others. It takes me a couple of turns to get to it and I lose it a few times, but I make it there with all of my favorite parts intact.

It's a passage, not even as wide as the one in the rocks, so I have to go in sideways. Once I'm through it, I can sort of see around me, but it's still pretty dark. Even a dim bulb would look bright here.

Off to my left, there's Puddler or Yeager, with his face to the wall and with his back to me, like a kid caught talking out of turn. And at the other end of the row is Yeager or Puddler, also showing off his haircut.

The chumps aren't exactly parrots in a cracker factory, but something about the silence is getting to me. I yell out "Hey, fellas," and they both move their shoulders like they're listening for what I might have to say next, but neither one turns around.

I say "Hey, fellas" again because my small talk seems to have shrunk, and this time, they start walking towards me, but without turning around to face me. Backwards, heels first.

They just keep getting closer and closer, but they don't turn around. Five feet away, and they're still facing away from me, walking on their heels.

I turn around, looking to take a powder, but I can't seem to find the way I came in. Just a solid wall. Puddler and Yeager keep getting closer and closer.

. . .

That's when I wake up for fair, on the floor at the foot of the bed, my pockets turned out and drool down my collar, with a headache you could see from the moon.

I feel like Humpty Dumpty on Easter—in a powder blue suit two sizes too small and cuffed almost to my knees and me broken to pieces with no one to put me back together again. I can only just barely breathe. The jacket feels like a third-rate wrestler that can't tell when the fix is in, and the pants pull in the crotch something awful. It's like wearing a slingshot while straddling a fence. If I could stand up, I'd check for Lozelle, but I don't seem to be able to get any push out of my arms or legs. I manage to scoot myself up the frame behind me and onto the bed before it's lights out again.

. . .

When I come to the second time, Brody's sitting across from me at the desk. He doesn't seem all that surprised to find me on the bed in the room. The poor sap looks worse than me, if that's possible, like somebody just stepped on his onliest puppy. He's holding up bags with bowling balls in

> *them under bloodshot eyes and he's hunched over like he's trying to touch his toes without bending at the waist. It's Brody all right, but not Brody, as it turns out.*

Brody came clean to Archer—he had been hired by an operator named General Norris Sternwood to feel out what Carmady knew about Steiner's racket. When word got back to the General that Carmady was purely on the outside looking in when it came to Steiner, Brody's card had been punched.

The General was a hard man to read, and Brody preferred the radio to books anyway. For some reason, the General had thought that Carmady might have some connection to Steiner, or to something that Steiner might have had that the General wanted. He didn't go any further than that, and Brody got off there. After all, Brody worked for the man at South Basin Oil Company and he was not in a position to say no or to ask stupid questions like "Why?"

Brody's real name was Goodridge Bowen, but he had been going by Julian Pascal ever since New York. As Pascal, he had moved out to Los Angeles hoping to score at least a club date or two, if not the movies, but it didn't take, and when the General, a friend of his wife's, offered him a paying gig, he couldn't afford to turn it down. Not if he wanted to keep his wife happy, and he desperately did want to keep her happy.

Trouble was, she wasn't happy. Not anymore. She had met someone, and even though her beau had slunk off to San Francisco without so much as a goodbye, she hadn't been able to get him off her mind—and Pascal hadn't been able to get her out of her pants—ever since.

[34]

When America's biggest farm town, Hollywood, was first incorporated, conmen imported from the East were the only operators working Farmer Whitley's orange groves. They were, one and all, in Southern California to chisel and cheat their way out of Edison's patents, and their businesses were here today, gone today, and sometimes back tomorrow, depending on how the moneymen back East felt about their latest reels. Funny thing about conmen, though, is that if they stay in business long enough, they stop being conmen and become just plain businessmen. Soon enough, all that movie moolah greened over the brown of Los Angeles's canyons and arroyos, making the whole enterprise look sane. And so it happened that the booming industries in Los Angeles in the twenties and thirties, the movies and real estate, were based on the shell games and grift of the naughts and the teens.

General Norris Sternwood had been there before the conmen. A veteran of the Spanish-American War twice decorated, the General found himself on the sharp's side in the original Southern California con: the land grab that turned a loose confederation of lazy Mexican rancheros into a loose confederation of lazy Yankee dude ranchers. He hadn't come to California to be a rancher—his service to his country had left him with a list of health problems nearly as long as his service record, and nearly as distinguished. The sunshine and dry climate agreed with him. He hired a man to raise the gentleman's crop, oranges, while he tended to himself and his rather healthier bank account. When a surveyor discovered oil on the General's sizable ranch, he founded South Basin Oil and watched his money triple, quadruple, and then multiply better than ten pages of the Bible, all without lifting a finger or anything else, either. Which was fortunate, because the General was in no shape to be lifting much of anything.

The General's choice of Southern California was prompted by a weakness for little girls that had drained both his bank account and his health reserves. He and his doctors thought that this desert on the edge of the Continent, in addition to providing dry air, warmth, and sunshine, would be well out of the path of harlots and gold-diggers, not to mention au pairs, B-girls, cigarette hustlers, debutantes, farmer's daughters, governesses, housewives, maids, nannies, sales girls, schoolgirls, schoolmarms, seamstresses, streetwalkers, taxi dancers, torch singers, dancehall wallflowers, war widows, and the rarest of them all, virgins, and they were right, right up until the arrival of Hollywood, when they all came flooding in. In the end, even the General wasn't immune to the wide open charms of America's Next Big Scheme, and when all was said and done, alimony had made him two million dollars poorer, he had had two daughters with two different mothers, and his health was worse than it had been before the move. The two million was a drop in the bucket—his taste in women was the real trouble.

Cissy Pascal had been lured to Los Angeles with a rod held by General Sternwood, and, reeled in, rendered some essential services to the old man, a fan of Cissy's since her dancehall days. In return, Julian Pascal was hired on at South Basin Oil, keeping her close and him closer. With the General's fading health, though, Cissy had slipped gracefully back into her role as housewife and Pascal had stopped wearing horns to work. He got a promotion, a raise. They got comfortable.

In the direction these things usually take, it wasn't long before a bouncing middle-aged boy named Raymond Chandler showed up on their doorstep, and Pascal didn't have the sense to shoo the stork. Chandler wasn't around long, just long enough, and when he lit out for San Francisco in 1927, he took along more than what was in his suitcase.

Two years later, Chandler returned from San Francisco the conquering hero, saving Pascal's skin by nailing Owen Taylor's hide to the wall. Even if Chandler had more designs on his wife than there are scenes from the Old Testament on a cathedral's windows, Pascal could hardly cast the first stone; he owed the guy that much. But Cissy hadn't been home to her husband in over a year, and when she didn't come home at all one night in January of 1929, he naturally thought of the jowly new accountant at South Basin. He tapped Chandler the next day.

Chandler got the General to promise Pascal some help with finding the old girl, and Pascal had been happy as two clams and a lark, happy enough that he was willing to smile on hiring an unlicensed detective and posing as another man to do it. The General couldn't have word getting around that his vice-president's wife was shacking up with known pornographers like Steiner. Made perfect sense to Pascal.

A week of working with Carmady had produced nothing, though, and the General told him that the case would have to be closed no matter what Carmady might turn up—Chandler had a line on whatever it was that the General wanted, and the General was cutting Carmady and Pascal loose. The poor sap lost it. He smashed up Steiner's, and the whole illusion shattered, like seven year's bad luck. The General said he had had the demo job hushed up to prevent his own name from coming out, but Pascal figured it was just another way to swing something heavy over his vice-president's head, should Pascal decide to buck him.

And Pascal was right. When he went up the hill on bended knee, the General gave him a choice: cut his losses or serve his time. Whichever he chose, Carmady and Steiner were out. So, it seemed, was Cissy. There were men sitting on Carmady's Boulevard office and South Basin secretaries listening in on Pascal's telephone, so he couldn't even give Carmady the word. He had only come to the Roosevelt tonight to grab the suit and make it official: Brody was dust. The fact that the cleaning crew had come through before him had to mean something, didn't it? Something bad. He used the phone in the lobby, and hoped that Carmady would be smart enough to dodge the two stooges the General had sicced on him.

> First the ventriloquist drops Sternwood's name on me, then Chandler's. He's pretty good at putting on the act, but he doesn't know when to bring down the curtain.

Usually, when the plot gets really kinky, Sherlock Holmes untangles it with a long, windy speech and a puff on the pipe. Pascal hasn't got a pipe, but I'm more interested in the wind anyway.

"Listen, Brody, Pascal, whatever your name is: if the General is half the guy you think he is, we all might be better off just letting sleeping dogs lie. Maybe the old girl found a new home after all. What if she did? It happens every day. This line of business, I see it all the time."

"You don't know my Cissy. She wouldn't. She isn't that type."

"All right, I'll bite. What type is she, Pascal? Your printing isn't exactly smudge-proof either, you know. You need to start playing according to Hoyle if you want me to throw my hand in. Lay them out."

"Well, Mr. Carmady, the truth is I did a little sleuthing before I went to you. The first night she didn't come home, I asked Chandler if he knew where she was. That's when he told me about Steiner and the shop. After work, when Cissy still hadn't come home, I drove down the Boulevard and bluffed my way into the backroom. That's where I got that picture of that woman I showed you."

"'That woman?' That wasn't your wife?"

"I don't know who she is, but I'm pretty sure that she was the same woman that Steiner had running his front room. She's wearing a wig in the picture, but I'm sure it's her. Maybe you could find her, ask her if she knows where Steiner's gone."

"Where Steiner's gone, I'm not following, Pascal. Skip it."

"But if Steiner knows where Cissy went . . ."

"It wouldn't do you any good now. Drop that line."

"Mr. Carmady—if Steiner knows where Cissy's gone, surely he's the man to talk to."

"He's not talking anymore. Look, Pascal, I know that you're not as dumb as you're playing me. You have Steiner's books. How did you know he wouldn't be looking for them? Who's this Geiger?"

"Geiger? Books? I don't know what you're talking about, Carmady. Honest I don't."

"Twelve packing crates full of dirty books were offloaded outside your door. I watched the man do it. Then I went downstairs and jawed with the clerk about your sleeping habits, and when I got back up here, they were gone but you were here. Explain that to me, Pascal."

"I can't. I don't know what you're talking about. I didn't tell anyone I was here. No one knows except for Chandler, and maybe

the General. Who would have sent me anything here, anyway?"

"That's your story?"

"I don't know any other to tell you, Carmady. Honest, I don't. I come here to change my clothes, that's all. I probably haven't spent more than an hour here in the two weeks since Chandler took it."

"Chandler again? You ought to throw in pretty high, Pascal, you've got one hell of a poker face . . . All right, skip it. You were about to tell me the one about a guy walking into a backroom. Suppose you finish that one."

"Steiner's? Well, the way I remember it, he was sitting at a desk next to the door, with those jeweler's glasses on, only with the right one blacked out. He was looking at a black statue, a statue of a bird. He had, let me see, he had one of those little hammers they use in one of his hands and I remember, he gave me a look like he was going to throw it at me. He told me to buy something or beat feet."

"A statue of a bird? What kind of a bird?"

"I don't know, a black one. Do you want me to finish the story or not? That's when I grabbed that picture off of a stack at the desk and asked if he had other pictures, pictures of other women. I described my wife to him. Steiner told me to take the picture and get

out. The next morning, I showed it to Chandler, and he went to the General. When he came back that afternoon, he had the whole thing planned out. They told me exactly where to go and what to say when I got there. They told me you would find my wife. They told me that Steiner had her, or knew where she was."

"And you bought Chandler's line, Pascal, signed, sealed, delivered? They let it out and reeled you in?"

"No. You see, Chandler showed me a mimeographed letter from Steiner to my wife. Apparently, he got his hands on some pictures of her, from before we met, pictures of her from when she worked . . . Well, when she worked as an artist's model, you know. She's not proud of that period, but, well, everyone has to make a living . . . She showed the letter to Chandler and told him that Steiner was threatening to go to the papers with these pictures. We'd be disgraced. I'd be out of a job. She'd have to quit her clubs. Even worse things might have happened, Carmady. Much worse things. Chandler said he warned her not to, but she went to Steiner's to get them back. That son-of-a-bitch did something with her, I know it."

"The papers couldn't print something like that. God knows they would if they could."

"Yes, but Chandler said that he had a few that were tame enough to print but still wild enough to get everyone in big trouble. After Cissy disappeared, Chandler told the General all about it. There was some talk that the General had been one of the clients in the photographs. That's why he wanted to go after Steiner, you see? Naturally, he couldn't do it himself . . . He has too much standing here in town. He'd be embarrassed, even if we found the pictures."

"But you said that Steiner wrote the letter to your wife, not to the General. Wouldn't it make more sense to shoot for the rod with the dough than the fish on the end of it?"

"I would appreciate it if you would be more careful when referring to my wife, Mr. Carmady. Anyway, I'm not a blackmailer; I don't know how it works. Maybe you do."

"Yeah, I do, and this isn't the way it works. This wrap stinks worse than the fish tale you came to me with a week ago. Only one thing hasn't changed: it's still the mermaid's fault."

"It's the truth, Mr. Carmady. The truth. Only it seems like the truth's not enough for you. Or is it the other way around?"

His face looked like a ruby soaked in beet juice, and his fists were clenched tight enough to crack walnuts. In one of them was a .38 that looked like it meant business, and business was booming.

"You've got me all wrong, Pascal."

He let the iron do the rest of his talking. I decided to let it have the last word.

[35]

Archer didn't get much more out of Pascal after the gat reared its ugly head: a look like you would give someone who's had their hand in your pocket on the streetcar and the old heave-ho. That, and another tail.

After crossing Orange, Archer caught a glimpse of Pascal in the glass of the El Capitan's coming attractions—*No, No, Nanette* and Pascal's puss waving like a flag as he hoofed his way through the usual plague of show-night locusts. Pascal was playing cool for the benefit of the pedestrians, trying to look like he wasn't tailing Archer and wasn't packing heat. He wasn't very good at either one. The crowd split like penguins around a seal.

Just before McCadden, Archer ducked into the diner to let Pascal pass. He took his usual booth in the window, right across from Geiger's shop, raised his finger for a cup of Java. Pascal never passed. Maybe he was biding his time at the shoeshine stand on the corner, or at the newsstand next to it. Could have been hiding under his grandmother's skirt, for all Archer knew, or tumbling down an open manhole. Archer didn't think much of the guy's shadowing skills, or his patience. Sooner or later, he would get nervous and beat it, and Archer could walk out in style, with a meal in his belly to boot.

When the girl came with the mud, he ordered a plate of hash. The fresh-off-the-farm types were all standing at the front, blocking Archer's view of Pascal's station. They were watching a scuffle outside on the sidewalk in front of the diner—two bits' worth of bums fighting over a quarter—and the scene took Archer's eye away from Geiger's window long enough that the light that had been on when he sat down had gone off when he looked back across the Boulevard, without him seeing the finger that had hit the switch.

> *No one shows outside the shop. Must have missed them—Pascal pulling that iron on me's got me bugged.*
>
> *Anyway, it's hard to tell from here, behind this glass front in the dark—could've been a light on in Geiger's, or it could have been a reflection from a spoon behind me, or even*

a stray headlamp on the Boulevard. Glass plays tricks on you like that.

Some Joe walks in the front door and elbows his way to the counter—not Pascal. I don't catch his face, but the suit's a pinstripe number with runners as wide as cigars. He looks like a color-blind zebra on his night off from the zoo.

One of the brawlers tries to push his way through into the diner, but the Joe behind the counter isn't having it. The other bum isn't done with him yet, anyway, and they go back to hammering out their differences until the bully squad shows up.

Los Angeles is a frontier town beyond the frontier, with no frontier beyond it. Any outpost where even the suckers are trying to get over is bound to be a rough place: too many dreamers, not enough dreams. Aside from the rascals' rumble outside of the Christie, police reports from that night log a loose cannon in the crowd at Mann's Chinese who almost set off a riot when he got mistaken for Wallace Beery. Must have been a hot night. A John Doe on Franklin got a lot more ink than either—it even made the front page of Harry Chandler's rag the next morning.

The two pugs on the Boulevard were nobodies in a town full of nobodies. Just shuffling feet and doughy faces. The only time a nobody breaks onto the front page is when he gets his pine box. Some lucky stiff every day of the week, some weeks. The beauty contest no one wants to win. In Santa Monica, an innocent wanders into a lead party; downtown, bootleggers in a panel truck, trying to slip the revenuers, run over a little old lady; crooked cops get the wrong gee in a shootout in Inglewood—the poor stiff dodges one red carnation only to get pinned by the people who are supposed to be saving him. Hell of a time to be alive.

When the coppers finally show and run off the riffraff, Archer sees that, while he's been watching windows, somebody has been watching him. The zebra at the counter has his spoon up and is moving it between his thumb and index like he's trying to pick up KNX inside of a bank vault. When he sees that he's made, the sly gets up to pay his bill. He stops to waste time at the dime novel rack next to the cashier's booth.

Something about the gee seems familiar, but Archer can't pick it out with the peeper's peepers knee deep in the paperback.

> Man in the Shadows, *by some desk-jockey named Carroll John Daly. I could even believe he's reading it, if not for the fact that he's holding it wrong side up.*
>
> *Wait a minute: it's Batzel! Why's Batzel giving me the eye?*

That's when Pascal decides to shoot the moon and walks past the diner's glass.

[36]

Before Archer can even drop his buck and a half on the table, Batzel is already crossing McCadden, tripping on Pascal's heels. And by the time Archer can feel a breeze, Batzel pushes past the velvet rope and stops Pascal in the middle of the opening-night crowd outside of the *Egyptian* (Archer has the feature down as G. W. Pabst's *Pandora's Box*) with a shoulder tap and a stage whisper. The crowd is the usual assortment of painted studio shills and savage beaded natives, all of them wondering when somebody who's anybody's going to get there. Nothing worse than getting what you paid for when you didn't have to pay anything for it. Archer crosses the Boulevard to skip the scalping and ducks back a couple of steps on Las Palmas to take in the powwow.

Plenty of jaw music, but since they're busy with the harps, they have to save the hoedown for after. Batzel takes the lead, and he sends Pascal spinning down the Boulevard like a seasick sailor looking for the rail. Not that that's so hard to do.

Still, not exactly ships in the night, these two.

Pascal didn't look surprised at the tap, just at what came out of it. Whatever that was, it must have been pretty damned important, considering how fast Pascal shakes it.

How does a lamming card sharp from Santa Monica know a washed up monkey-suit man working a desk in Hollywood?

Batzel's in the crowd one minute and gone the next. I'll see him in 24 anyway.

Despite the .38 and the San Francisco squint, I figure it might be worth my while to keep on Pascal, on the off chance that his actions speak louder than his words, or at least, talk turkey a lot more often.

Pascal stopped at Schrader, waiting for the traffic to tell him whether to cross the Boulevard or not. In the end, he ignored it and jumped a passing eastbound.

Archer hoofed it after the trolley, trying to keep close enough to spot passengers stepping off at Cahuenga. He was probably hoping to make his jalopy before the car made the horizon, but he was pulled up short by a brown Packard stopped in the middle of the intersection at Wilcox. Batzel was behind the wheel, and the passenger door was open.

> *"Sorry Charlie, but I haven't got time to chitterchat. I'll see you tomorrow at eight."*
>
> *"Well, Mr. Carmady, you see, this isn't exactly an accidental meeting. You might say I rang up this little run-in. You might even say I've been holding the line just for you."*
>
> *"Yeah, I might, but don't hold your breath. Listen, Batzel, I'm on the hook for another line . . ."*
>
> *"If you mean Pascal, I'm afraid that exchange will be out of order from now on. But don't worry, old sport. It won't matter, in the end."*
>
> *"How's that?"*
>
> *"Mr. Pascal has been taken care of. If you'll kindly step in, I'll explain it as we go, Mr. Carmady. Or should I call you Marlowe, Marlowe?"*
>
> *"You know an awful lot for a faro dealer, Batzel. Too much if you ask me."*
>
> *"I'm afraid I'll have to insist. It seems there are others waiting."*
>
> *The line of geese went all the way up Wilcox to Yucca.*

"Meter's running, Marlowe. Get in." Batzel showed lead, and I stepped in. I couldn't see the streetcar anymore anyway.

"I rather like Marlowe. I'm sure it suits you better. And, please, call me Ray. Everyone else does. Ray Chandler."

Chandler. Pascal's eight ball. The soggy pants coin-counter who seems to have all the angles bent on the General's table.

"You're the squeaky wheel down at South Basin. Pascal's squeaky wheel."

"Yes, I suppose so. But I won't need any further greasing. From Pascal, anyway."

"No? Who's Larry Batzel, Chandler?"

"Oh, he's just a character I invented. A necessary evil. A half-smart guy, as you might say. I hadn't given him that much thought really."

"What about Santa Teresa, the job?"

"Well, that's real enough, Marlowe. I don't suppose you've been up there yet?"

"Too much company."

"Yes, Puddler and Yeager. Rather overzealous, I'm afraid. It seems to have caught up with them, though. I can assure you, you won't have any more problems with them."

"What's that supposed to mean?" Chandler swung the Packard west on Sunset, then *back north on Highland, making a lazy circle around the Christie like a dog putting on its pajamas. He was hunched over toward me studying the street signs like he was afraid they were going to change names on him.*

"Look, Chandler, I like bed-time stories as much as the next guy, but tell me one with a beginning middle and end."

"Sure, Marlowe, sure. How about the one about the ivory-tickler who outsmarted himself?"

"I'm listening."

"Once upon a time, there was a boy who didn't exist. This boy's name was Julian Pascal. You see, I'm afraid that, as far as the law goes, only Goodridge Bowen exists, through a rather unfortunate clerical error made when Mr. Bowen decided to change his name to Julian Pascal. And when Mr. Bowen brought his bride-to-be to the justice of the peace and gave the name Julian Pascal, and then went on to sign the marriage certificate with the name Julian Pascal, well, you see, it was as if no one at all had signed it, no one at all had been married. In the eyes of the law, no one had been married. And so, ten years later, when the woman who wasn't his wife discovered that she had fallen in love with someone else, someone who was willing to use his

real name on the marriage certificate, why, it was just as easy as if Julian Pascal had never existed at all."

"Are you saying that you and Cissy are married?"

"Celebrated our nuptials yesterday, as a matter of fact."

"And that's what you told Pascal?"

"That and a whole lot more. You might say I rubbed him out; I erased him. I simply told him the truth: that he never existed to begin with. I believe he was on his way to City Hall, but then, of course, they're closed. Anyway, they can't help him. Funny how a little thread like that can unravel a person's whole life."

"All right, Chandler. What about the two church bells, Puddler and his partner?"

"Yeager? They might seem hard as brass, but they're as human as you or I. They get frustrated when things don't go the way they're supposed to. Seems they lost their patience with a certain suit that didn't live up to its lining."

"What suit? Brody, I mean, Malvern? What are you saying, Chandler? What happened to Malvern?"

"I'm saying that Mr. Malvern, as you call him, is no longer with us, and the men who put him under glass are behind bars now.

You know, Marlowe, it's true what they say: crime doesn't pay. Certain crimes, anyway. Others pay quite a lot. Quite a lot indeed."

I didn't like the way he was looking at me. I didn't like the way he tied Pascal and Malvern, Puddler and Yeager up in pretty little bows. I didn't like his suit and I didn't like his voice, I didn't even like his breath. He looked like a forty-year old twelve-year old, one who spends his afternoons tearing the wings off flies and then pasting them into a scrapbook. Snips, snails, and puppy dog tails.

Big boys like Chandler make big messes, and never clean them up. If not for guys like him, guys like me would never make a dime, but that doesn't mean I have to like it. Or him.

[37]

North of the Boulevard, Chandler showed Archer his Coney Island Cyclone version of the Hollywood Hills. Turned out, the streets were only dead ends if you kept to the pavement. After the last named street had been crested, Chandler turned out the headlamps and the Packard dropped into a canyon.

> *There aren't any city lights out here and it would be impossible to tell where we were even if it was twelve noon—none of these roads has a name and most of them aren't even roads—but with Chandler's chinning about pictures and parties, it wouldn't surprise me if we were on our way to Steiner's.*
>
> *Chandler's telling me about his time up in San Francisco, but every couple of beats, the*

bumps in the track swallow whatever word he's chewing on, and I lose the taste. Two out of three ain't bad, unless you're keeping track. There's no track here to keep to, so I guess I'm all right just ignoring him, concentrating on my motion sickness. Chandler doesn't take his foot off the gas, not even when he's turning.

The night outside is like the other side of the moon, with a few stars showing at the top of the canyon to tell us when we're getting too close to the grade, but this skipper's not steering a landau: we can only see the lights that are far enough away not to get blocked out by the Packard's roof. Chandler steers pretty straight between the walls of the canyon but every now and again we hit a swell and Chandler has to yank the car back into the middle using his whole body.

When we run aground on some scrub, Chandler switches off the wireless at the back of his throat and turns the wheel to the right. He guns the engine, but the tires just spin in the loose dirt. Chandler keeps his foot on the gas and gives the open-sesame loud and clear, and we shoot forward about twenty yards. He turns the wheel the other way, and we go another twenty yards or so.

After a few more turns and a lot more curses, the Packard fights the slope and Chandler fights the Packard and we rear up.

The night opens up all around us, like a big black orchid, with the tiny white eyes of the city on the petals.

I hate orchids. They smell like rotting meat. Chandler's car doesn't smell too much better.

Chandler slams on the brakes at the very top of the rise.

"Beautiful, isn't it Marlowe? What it would look like without all of the people. Just empty buildings with all the lights left on." Then he drops the car off the other side, and everything's black again. A couple more turns that I can't keep track of and Chandler slams the jalopy into park at the foot of a flight of steps leading up into more darkness.

"All right, Marlowe. I've got some things to show you. Just a few mementos—pictures, really. But I think you'll be interested. You don't have a choice anyway."

Even in the dark I can see the iron flashing. Steiner's house. I was right. Still no light to see by, but the steps are broken in the right places: I go right through the splintered one, landing hard enough on the next step down to snap it in two, and I'm only saved from making like Jack and tumbling back down the side of the canyon by the sleeve of Malvern's jacket, which catches on the rail and splits down to the armpit. I hear Chandler up ahead, laughing at me to beat the band.

What's he got up his sleeve?

Up Chandler's sleeve was a list of plots long enough to make a studio script-doctor, or a magician in search of a handkerchief, jealous, and a knack for mixing them up. That, and a few pictures.

[38]

The pictures that Chandler showed Archer that night are still in Chandler's South Basin files, mixed in with a few photos of some John in an orange grove—the gee's facing away from the camera in all of them. Chandler wasn't dumb enough to label the file "Sternwood Blackmail Pics," but from Archer's descriptions in the notebook, we can be pretty sure which vacation slideshow Chandler put on for him in Steiner's cabin.

The first is a picture of the falcon. The real one, the one that wound up in the SFPD evidence locker. It's the standard-issue evidence photo, complete with evidence tag at the bottom right. The bird is a black statuette, wings folded and beak in profile, solid, dark, and with a flat finish that looks like it's been scratched and repainted more than once. The evidence tag is blank: no numbers, no letters. Who knows how the pic was filed, or even if it was filed.

> *Chandler leaves me in the empty living room and disappears into the garage. He comes back with the big black book and an envelope, and shows me the top pic from the envelope, a frontal of the falcon. What I don't get is, if he knows it was me in San Francisco, why not just come right out and say it? He would have evidence in the way of receipts from the old agency, and I'd be dead to rights, if no longer legally dead.*
>
> *And if he doesn't make me from San Francisco, is he as smart as he's playing, or just lucky?*

Chandler was either smart or lucky, because the second pic is also of the falcon, but not from the SFPD file. In this one, the falcon's on its back, with the base facing the camera. And—surprise, surprise—the falcon's guts have spilled. The hollow in the middle of the falcon is empty—whatever cargo it was carrying has been unloaded. If Archer had his suspicions before about the falcon's density, he wouldn't have after he saw this pic.

There's no mention of what the bird was carrying, either in Archer's notes or in Chandler's files. The photos that follow, though, give the clue. Keyhole snaps, nasty ones, of a honeymoon suite in the process of being christened. Hubby's bottle of bubbly is just about to spray the hull of the newly-renamed ship in the last of the series. Despite a good look at the bottle and its bucket, though, the prow of the vessel is just out of view, a face more question than answer, and there are gaps in the sequence of snaps where the siren's figurehead might have peeked into the frame. Probably, given what followed, the blushing bride was Carmen Sternwood. But, whoever it was on the receiving end, the fellow doing the giving looked an awful lot like General Norris Sternwood.

[39]

Archer couldn't have picked the General out of a lineup of Eskimos and Africans, but Chandler assured him that the old man in the photo was indeed the General. And the young lady in the photos was almost certainly one of the General's daughters, though which daughter, he wasn't entirely certain: they looked alike. Most of the rest was hogwash, with Chandler doing the oinking and the rinsing. He told Archer he had got word of the photos about a week before: a blackmailer, later identified as Steiner, had sent teasers to the Sternwood household, care of "Ms. Sternwood," but he had intercepted them. Chandler explained that he had the dubious distinction of opening and occasionally responding to the Sternwoods' mail. Archer had his doubts.

The family business worked fine as a crowbar, but Archer had to play dumb on the falcon angle or else risk getting caught out in his own tall tale. Archer asked Chandler what the falcon had to do with the price of grapes in Greece, and Chandler told him an iron fist in a velvet glove named Eddie Mars, on the hunt for the falcon when it was turned over to the police back in San Francisco, had managed to slip the bird out of its cage with a Bess made of greenbacks. Mars had had it brought down to Los Angeles, but he couldn't get the bird to fly. Chandler, being wise, could, but couldn't seem to get his mitts on the bird. He thought he had that wrapped up when he fingered Mars at the Cypress Club, but the bird flew away again before he could get the hood on it.

Eddie Mars, Chandler told Archer, was flabby as a wet towel dipped in melted soap, like a giant blob of walking, talking gravy—a balding man of average height and above average width, with a map of the Spice Islands in liver spots high on his forehead, eyes like raisins in oatmeal, a nose like a rotting eggplant, and an appetite like a prize-fighter. He was also one of the Cypress Club's main backers, and the big cheese at so many suppers it would take a grocery list as long as the dictionary to list them all.

Mars had bent the bars on the falcon's cage, and rode the bird down to Los Angeles, on the advice of his second-in-command, Mesarvey, who drew his falcon feather from the same quiver Chandler did—Carmen Sternwood. Back at the St. Francis, Carmen had told Mesarvey, then in disguise as Joel Cairo, only that she wanted the falcon and would pay for it. She let Chandler in on the secret by accident: after walking together on the homicide in Burritt Alley, and before Chandler could motor her back to her father in Los Angeles, she bunked with the bankman at his apartment in San Francisco, and spilled the beans in her sleep.

Chandler had also got wind of the falcon's reappearance from Carmen, who started to bring Cypress Club vouchers directly to Chandler at South Basin, looking for the handout to hand over to Mesarvey for safe return of the bird. Chandler had gone to the Cypress Club as Batzel and worked the floor for a couple of nights to see if he could clap his eyes on the flighty fowl. He finally did, in transit to Steiner's Boulevard shop, and managed to sweet talk a B-girl working the Cypress Club's bar into opening her legs for Mars and his silent partner, Steiner, and walking away with more than just a social disease.

But he made two mistakes. First, he didn't show at the club the next night, or any night after. A rookie mistake, the kind of slip-up that little boys playing cops and robbers might let slide, but, when they get some hair on their chests, rates them a dirt-nap. Mesarvey fingered the invisible man behind the heist, and sent Puddler and Yeager after him. When they came up Victor Fleming on the search for Batzel, Mars made some changes at the Cypress Club: Puddler and Yeager got a room with no view downtown, and Mesarvey went into the fertilizer business.

The second mistake was Chandler's choice for a stash. Chandler had tapped Betty Fraley, a B-girl with a B face, a cocaine nose, and no future or conscience, for the swipe, never dreaming that the bim would get wise to the way the falcon worked. She did, and Chandler got another note with snaps attached, trying to sink a line into him and the man in the photographs, whoever that was. She might not have known anything about the big fish, but she knew that Chandler wanted the pictures back—bad—and that they were valuable enough to hide them in a lead bird.

[40]

The design behind the pics was easy enough to guess: not even an oil tycoon with a private Fort Knox could buy his way out of an immorality charge with real weight behind it, but he could sure as hell try. He might be able to afford the paper they were printed on, might even be able to afford to keep the blackmailers' mouths shut. But if they ever got out, his name wouldn't be worth the deed it was printed on.

From the process and the paper, it looks like the snaps were printed a year or so before Archer hit Los Angeles, around 1927, when Carmen Sternwood would have been just 17, and her sister, Vivian, 21. In the spring of 1927, there are a couple of *Times* society-page shots of General Sternwood setting off from New York on a round-the-world trip with his two daughters. Carrying one of the girl's steamer trunks aboard the *R.M.S. Aquitania* is a young Floyd Thursby, alias Dan Wallace, fingered as Owen Taylor in the photo's caption. Also in the photo, though partly hidden by the framing, are Ralph Sampson and a young woman very likely his daughter, Penelope.

The décor of the room in the photos hidden in the falcon places them at the then-just-finished Megaron Hotel, on the island of Crete; in its day, the Ritz Hotel of Heraklion. The itinerary for the Sternwoods' European jaunt puts them there, too; if that was just a coincidence, it's a bull whale of a coincidence. They sailed from Piraeus on the 18th of May, and left the island, headed for Constantinople, six days later, on the 24th. But Sternwood had his mail forwarded to the Megaron for eleven days, scheduled to end on the 29th of May, and missed the delivery of a letter from Los Angeles informing him of a derrick fire. A careless spark from the drilling equipment's rusted bore set off the blaze, and in just two hours, a month's worth of crude was burnt. The housing was also ruined, and the equipment. That particular derrick would never pump oil again.

Whatever caused the General to skip town, it didn't prevent him from returning to the Megaron on the way back, when he caught up with the missing correspondence and discovered the destroyed derrick. It was one of the last pumping on the grounds of the Sternwood estate, less than a hundred yards from the South Basin Oil offices, which were providentially unharmed by the massive conflagration. The General cut short the planned Italian leg, and the Sternwoods headed for home.

On their return, a name started to appear with more and more frequency in South Basin's account books, circling like a sharkfin in a soup tureen: "O'Mara Investigations," a front that Eddie Mars ran as a sideline to his other sidelines, as far as Chandler could tell. Mars's deliverymen ferried spirits ship-to-shore from Mexican and Canadian vessels and into the backrooms and closets of the rich and the famous. While they were there, they poked around for skeletons and usually found them. The "investigations" were pure geology: seeing how deep the customers' pockets went. The deeper the well, the more you could pump out of it.

For all that, Mars would have been just the bird-watcher to tap for the locale of the falcon's nest; any foreign fowl washing up on California's beaches, and Mars was bound to have a line on it. The amounts of the checks are small enough and frequent enough to cover a dick's expenses, smaller grabs than Chandler would have expected from the black hand, with corresponding spikes when the bird touched down in San Francisco and, briefly, in Santa Monica. He was more than a little worried that the General's enemies might just turn out to be his employees after all. As he well knew, it definitely worked the other way around.

[41]

Fraley had slid into Steiner's pocket as easy as a cannon's hand on a Boulevard streetcar. She had the kind of sleazy charm he and his customers were looking for. But when it came to the falcon, Fraley told Chandler, things went as smoothly as a cat's tongue on sandpaper. She had it, sure, but she wanted to keep it in its cage for a little while longer, make sure Chandler wouldn't double-cross her. She sent him to clean up Steiner's house, clean out Steiner's stock. Then she posted the envelope; there was more. There was always more.

The invoice Fraley included with the pics showed only an address, no price tag or prospectus. Chandler was worried she might be holding back on him, keeping the best—or the worst—for herself, once she glommed what he did with the recovered booty. He had boarded Carmady's ship to check up on that for him, see who was backing her play. Or so he said.

> "That's all fine and dandy, Chandler: good enough for a page-two byline or one hell of a letter home. Let me guess: Fraley's address is the one you gave me way back when you were Batzel, I was Carmady, and the world was young?"
>
> "Yes, it is. Sharp, aren't you, Marlowe? That is precisely where the exchange was supposed to take place. But can you guess who called my office at South Basin just before I left today? That's right, Miss Fraley. I have reason to believe that she has a new partner—or rather, an old one. Not even bright enough to realize it's the same party she took it from in the first place. I should have known better."
>
> Chandler's either feeding me a line as wide as the San Francisco Bay, or he's in over his head. When coincidences start to pile up, it usually means that they're not coincidences. The whole thing could be a shell game with Mars (or Malvern, or a hundred other gees in the rackets) behind the table, a honey trap for busy bees like Chandler who get themselves in deep without their diving bells.
>
> "You mean Mars."

"Yes, I'm afraid so. It's too much of a coincidence: Santa Teresa's his town. Just after Mr. Fitts's secretary called to tell me they had Puddler and Yeager in custody, Miss Fraley called to say that she wanted to meet tomorrow, not Wednesday, as we had originally planned. Asked me to bring rather a lot of cash. Word does tend to get around, of course, but that's faster than a tortoise riding a hare, don't you think? With his two goons in the slammer, Mars must be desperate. Maybe he showed his hand to Miss Fraley. Maybe she liked it better than what I've been offering."

"Maybe. Or maybe he just told her what the bird is worth. Listen, before I go any further down your primrose path, and while I've got you answering questions and not just making them up, where's Steiner, Chandler?"

"Harold Steiner. Let's just say he's someplace safe."

"No, let's say where he is, and then let's say what part you have planned for me. I get a feeling like you already have me cast. I'd like to know my lines."

"You see? I told you you were sharp. Steiner's taking a little nap. That doesn't, however, mean that he won't wake up and resume his place here, where the two of you first met. It just means that, if you would prefer he took a walk down to the beach,

maybe a little dip instead, well, I think you can guess what you have to do, Marlowe."

"Sing 'Puttin' On the Ritz' in my best Harry Richman? Or maybe he doesn't go in for the talkies? He is being awful quiet."

"By all means, keep joking, Marlowe. I must say, you're quite a cut-up. But while you're thinking up your little jokes, you might also be thinking very clearly about how you want the next twenty-four hours to go. I'm afraid that your vaudeville act won't do you much good with the boys in blue. I am being, as you might say, dead serious."

"Maybe more than you know, Chandler. But don't forget, Steiner's the dead one."

"It could be catching." He had his gat in his right hand and the bullets he said were mine in his left. His look said he was going to get some use out of one or the other.

"Fine, but I didn't have anything to do with Steiner while he was alive, and I've got even less to do with him now he's dead. You know it and I know it."

"Perhaps so. Unfortunately, these bullets say otherwise, and the General has any number of fingermen on staff. Besides, you're living on borrowed time already, isn't that right, Carmady?"

"Why not stick with the plan, run up there yourself, Chandler, if all I'm doing is making

a handoff? Why do you need me? This Fraley bim knows you, right, she's in this racket with you? Why would she hand the snaps over to a stranger?"

"Hmm. Well, the truth is, I'm being followed. Why we had to run without lights back there. Whoever it is, they won't bother with you when they see you're alone. I'll take care of that. It's all quite simple. You shouldn't need to converse much, and so long as you keep your hat low and your collar high . . . I've still got the suit that I used at the Cypress Club. You see, you and I are about the same size and shape; it's why I went with you and not poor old Pascal—oh, and by the way, the suit you have on . . . really, Marlowe, it doesn't suit you at all. You see? You're not the only one who can turn a phrase: 'suit' doesn't 'suit.' Pretty good, hmm?"

"I've seen better cracks in the sidewalk. Wait a minute, how can I drop your tail if I'm dressed as you?"

"Well, you'll just have to change on the ferry. Or in Santa Monica. It's a blue Ford coupe, just the driver. The man looks familiar, but I've never seen him up close, so I'm afraid I don't have a description for you. Just make sure he isn't around when you get on the ferry, or we'll both be sunk. Come on, we'd better go, before someone spots these lights."

We went out the way we had come in: in the dark. It was a hell of a lot harder getting out, and it took longer, too. Chandler took a couple of left turns, a few right turns, and a lot of wrong turns. He laid down more of his bedtime story along the way, maybe hoping that I'd fall asleep.

"Miss Fraley is much more resourceful than I would have imagined. She's almost certainly the one with the man 'tailing' me, as you would say. It's what I would do, if I were in her shoes . . . damn!"

I noticed his eyes in the rearview and turned my head just enough to catch a silhouette in a dark coupe behind a pair of headlamps, about a block behind us on Highland.

"Your blue coupe, Chandler?"

"Yes. How could . . . How could he possibly have found us? He couldn't have been behind us in the canyons."

"You tail someone long enough, you know where they're going to be before they do. Looks to me like he's been on you for a while."

"We can't risk him pinning your new office, Marlowe. The less he knows about you, the better. I'll try to keep him busy while you make a break for it. First, though, my suit."

We pulled around to the rear entrance of the Roosevelt. The blue coupe had stopped in front of a hydrant at Selma. No one got out.

Chandler gave the doorman the cold shoulder and held the door open for me.

Inside, the old geezer that had me pegged as Brody was working the desk. But he spotted Chandler first, nodded. Chandler moved over to the desk.

"Is my suit ready?"

"Yessir, Mr. Brody. Brought it up to your suite just a moment ago . . ."

He stopped when he spotted me.

"I . . ."

"In the room? Fine. This is for you."

I touched my nose and nodded. The old man couldn't think what to say, and Chandler and I boarded the elevator. Claude barely batted an eyelash.

"Mr. Brody, good evening sir." He was looking at me, but Chandler answered.

"Fourth floor, please."

"Yessir, Mr. Brody. Going up."

It was quiet as a theater after the lights go down, all the way up to four. Chandler and I walked down the hall to 413, and Chandler got out his key.

"So you're Brody, too, huh Chandler?"

"Yes. And no. Someone had to rent this suite, for reasons that Pascal didn't need to know. Steiner's inventory, you see? I just told him it was a good place to get changed. Good enough for him. You'll have to find some other place, though, while I take care of the man downstairs."

He handed me a suit that was one part suit, three parts putting green. It looked like a chameleon tracking down a fly in the outfield of Comiskey Park.

"This is Batzel, huh?"

"This is Batzel. It's what all the debonair dealers are wearing this year."

"If you say so, Chandler. What about the ransom? Or am I just supposed to use my charm? Or should I say, your charm?"

"Waiting for you in your new office. A brown paper parcel. I must ask you to refrain from opening it, of course, but you may rest assured that it will meet with Miss Fraley's unqualified satisfaction. She was very specific about what she wanted and in what form it was to be delivered, and any tampering from you would . . . unnecessarily complicate things."

Business over, Chandler tells me to watch out the window until his Packard and the blue coupe pass by on the Boulevard below.

I take the stairs this time.

. . .

The package was where he said it would be. I didn't exactly have to overheat the old echo chamber to figure out how he got in. Sam, the droopy customer in the lobby, asked me if I needed his key again, or if I had found my own. I told him I had found it.

[42]

Before the gleam in H. J. Whitley's eye could reflect the cheap glamour and easy coin that is now Tinseltown, there was another dream factory about one hundred miles up the coast from Los Angeles: the American Film Manufacturing Company, better known to locals as The Flying A Studio. The Flying A was the biggest game in town, which wasn't saying much for a little ranch town like Santa Teresa, but for a few years, it was also the biggest game in the state. Peons showed up on Santa Teresa's doorsteps like an Egyptian plague, and the locals treated them accordingly. At that time, the Flying A was turning out more two-reelers than all of the Los Angeles studios combined. But when talkies came to town, Flying A took a flying leap off the ocean cliffs, and Santa Teresa went from boomtown to ranch town quicker than a Boulevard news vendor closing up for the night.

The only people left there were the people who didn't have to work to make a living, and the people who could make some kind of living off of those people. Santa Teresa had its share of gentleman ranchers and Los Angeles's and San Francisco's, too, and they all liked it that way.

Then, in June of 1925, an earthquake with a magnitude of 6.3 crumpled downtown Santa Teresa like a company man reading his pink slip. The wise city fathers decided to rebuild, on a civic plan that would have made a naval base look like a crazy quilt designed by the residents of a lunatic asylum. Red slate roofs and sandstone as far as the eye could see, enough to make even Leland Stanford, Jr. jealous, with height ordinances and landscaping regulations that made sure that everything looked just like everything else. By 1929, you needed a plat map just to turn a corner—every building looked the same, and every street name ended in either "a" or "o." Those wise city fathers had reclaimed their heritage, or, at least, they had borrowed one from the same people they borrowed their land from. They never gave either one back.

The new Santa Teresa was laid out so that every street turned into only one other, more a map for a tram system than a downtown: every few blocks, the streets were sliced in two by plazas or tree stands or some other obstruction. Only one outlet led out of the downtown to La Playa, the boulevard that ran along the cliffs above the ocean, which made it easy to make sure that only the right people got in, and even easier to keep an eye on the wrong people. On the ocean side, there was a steep flight of steps cut into the cliffs leading down from a path that ran along the boulevard, and a thin beach that disappeared when the tide came in. On the other side of town, the north side, were the Santa Ynez Mountains, as steep as a used car salesman's pitch, with not a single pass cut through to the valley beyond. Life in Santa Teresa was as placid as a prison cell, and twice as secure. It was the kind of town you never left, even if you wanted to. Fortunately for those wise city fathers, few people wanted to.

There was a long-haul car ferry from Santa Monica up to the next town over, Goleta, where you could catch the paved road that turned into La Playa, but otherwise, the air-strip in the foothills of the Santa Ynez was the only avenue in or out until the Pacific Coast Highway annexed La Playa in the mid-1930s. The small, private planes that made the trip overcharged accordingly.

For every millionaire with money to feed a dozen nags good for nothing but eating and glue, there were half a dozen gangsters holed up in the neighboring dude ranches or in one of a dozen downtown hostelries that catered to the trade. All of them private citizens, all intent on remaining private, and all with similar reasons.

The police force serving Santa Teresa County was bought and paid for to ride their horses, smile for the occasional camera, and clean up any messes that those horses or the citizens might make while walking *their* streets, just like good little stable boys. As long as everyone, rancher or gangster, did their business out of town, there was nothing more uplifting for them to do, and they were glad to not do it. Police forces from down south usually didn't have the wherewithal to make it all the way up to Santa Teresa, and that was just the way Santa Teresa's citizens liked it.

[43]

Of Santa Teresa's private citizens, the most private was Ralph Sampson, a jack-of-all-trades-master-of-none who had played more positions than an Abbott and Costello routine—most of them more comfortable on a rap sheet than a resume. Somewhere between gentleman and gangster, Sampson was one of the richest men in Santa Teresa, but he stacked his bills on black ink and bootleg liquor.

According to his own crooked tales, Sampson had come west to San Francisco from Illinois at the tender young age of thirty-five, leaving behind a skin-and-bones family and a whole lot of dust when the drought of 1898 killed all but one mangy heifer on his one-horse cattle ranch. He spent the next seven years on the streets of the Barbary Coast making something like a living as a roustabout, a tough guy, even a performer, when opportunity knocked. Apparently, Sampson was not without talent: he was known in the dives of old San Francisco as the One-Eyed Worm, and not because he was missing an eye. He took his tiny stake and opened a cathouse named Delilah's, painted yellow with white slaves just off the boat from Canton, in a converted stable at the corner of Jackson and Stockton. Delilah's burned to the ground in one of the blazes that turned the Barbary Coast into barbecue in the aftermath of the earthquake of 1906, and Sampson never again showed the entrepreneurial spirit.

At least, not officially: the black cloud hung over Sampson just a little too low and a little too full for a man who from that point forward apparently never wasted a day in his life working. He must have had something going for him—something good, something rich—just to have survived.

Sampson married Fay Estabrook, a former employee of Delilah's and the rare American there, the same year the pink parlor burned down. Estabrook was one of Florenz Ziegfeld's original follies, and a great favorite of none other than General Norris Sternwood, recently retired from the United States Army and just beginning to sow his wild oats after years of gathering his seed. Estabrook could barely carry a parasol, much less a tune, but she was shrewd enough to latch on to the General's arm. They toured the Continent together, kept up a Park Avenue townhouse, living the high life a little too high and a little too often for the General, a broken man after San Juan Hill and a bout of yellow fever. When his health failed again and he headed west, she followed. But the General hadn't left a forwarding address, and she wound up with Ralph Sampson instead.

The Sampsons had a daughter, Penelope, soon after they tied the knot. Too soon, for a newlywed suite conception. Penelope's birth certificate has a blank line next to the item "Father," but gives her full name as "Penelope Ann Sternwood." The last name is too coincidental to be accidental, but might have been written in for any number of reasons having nothing to do with ancestry and everything to do with blackmail. For all that, it just might be true. Guilt can move mountains, but grief rarely does. Money, on the other hand, can move whole island chains, especially in quantities like General Sternwood was holding. Fay died in childbirth, and the next year, Sampson bought a ranch in Santa Teresa and a stake in the Cypress Club.

Sampson had learned a thing or two about what to show and what to conceal from his employees at Delilah's: he signed the deed on the ranch Ralph Sampson but he bought into the Cypress under the name Eddie Mars. As Sampson, he held the occasional high society party, sent his Penny off to finishing school, had servants and a reputation. As Mars, he put his thumb in every pie in the Southland, from Santa Teresa to San Diego. He was the man behind the man, as well as the man in front, and he made sure that those men never met, in company or on paper.

But when two men on their way to the same place, both coming from the same small town—a small town by no means easy to leave undetected—go missing on the same day, it raises some flags.

And besides, the original touch, General Norris Sternwood, knew there was a connection. After all, he had been paying to maintain it for quite some time.

[44]

Archer had a night just like any other night, which is to say, he doesn't leak a line about it in the notebook. He ditches Malvern's duds, collects the General's package, and motors to Santa Monica, all in time to throw a cup of joe and a plate of hash down his gullet before jumping on the morning car ferry up the coast to Goleta.

> *I put the Batzel suit on at the station in Goleta. If Malvern's suit made me feel like a Dalmatian in a dollhouse, Chandler's puts me in the mirror: like a doll in a doghouse. Pascal in this getup would have been wearing the Emperor's new clothes in no time flat.*
>
> *I could probably fit another one of me in here, and I could use the company: there's*

only two other customers on the ferry —a police cruiser from Los Angeles and a fancy British touring car—and nobody at all on the road to Santa Teresa. No blue coupes, no grey coupes, no coupes at all. Just me, my jalopy, and a whole lot of ocean.

Santa Teresa from the ocean road is nothing but slate and stucco, a Spanish-style sanitarium. I haven't even got out of the car yet, but I can already tell: it's not my kind of town.

Back before I got to the red and white man-made cliffs of downtown Santa Teresa, there were at least a few gravel drives leading uphill off the paved road; ranches so bare they looked like someone put a wet newspaper on a radiator and left it there overnight.

The address Chandler had given me as Fraley's was one of them. It was dust and gravel for about a hundred yards, until you came to an open cattle gate where the road took a sharp S around a couple of hills. On the other side of the hills, the gravel got tony and so did the land. There was a line of eucalyptus trees on either side of the drive, and at the end, set back on a lawn the size of Asia Minor, the Taj Mahal of ranch houses, behind a set of gates that would keep out Alexander and his elephants. There weren't any cars at the house and no one watering the lawn, so the hour or so I spent there got me nothing but an empty stomach. I decided to see what dirt I could get on the ranch and Miss Fraley in town.

But by the time you spot the stucco of downtown Santa Teresa, there's not a speck anywhere, not even a wet newspaper. Nothing at all except for some lonely asphalt, a thin stripe of lonely white paint, and a lonely cafe advertising "EATS," and pouting like nobody believes it.

I park the coupe at EATS and walk across the boulevard into town. I don't even have to look both ways. The only car around is the one I just got out of.

There's a dark alley about the width of a wheelbarrow across from EATS. At the other end of the rabbit hole, the streets of downtown Santa Teresa look like no one's had occasion to use them yet. Maybe it's just that nobody's been able to find them.

No traffic to speak of. No cars. With the layout of the streets, I'm not too surprised about that. But no strollers? No long-lunchers? No teenagers? Not even a tumbleweed of newsprint along the gutter?

If stucco had eyes, I couldn't feel more looked at. Like falling into the tiger cage at the zoo, only you don't see the tiger. And you get the sneaking suspicion that you're the only one, and you wish that someone up there would please speak up. It's beginning to look a lot like I drove into town for nothing at all, and that's exactly what I got.

I keep my eyes peeled for the paper, maybe a police station—at the very least, a shoeshine or a newshawk with his hand out. If Fraley's stopping at King Solomon's farmhouse back there, somebody knows about it, and probably everything else there is to know about her, right down to her shoe size and how she likes her eggs.

Santa Teresa has an attorney's, a doctor's, a property agent's that isn't open, a dentist's, a pharmacist's, and a very closed library, but no paper. No police station. No shoeshine box. No news vendor.

I can't even find a cup of joe in this town. The pharmacist's is closed—judging from the dust in his window display, he's been on vacation for a few years.

I wonder what soda-jerks do for a living in this burg.

Hell, I wonder what pharmacists do for a living in this burg.

Takes me the better part of an hour, but I finally locate the sheriff's office, at the bend where La Loma becomes La Piedra.

Sheriff here is Albert Graves, either the movie star or somebody with the same name. The desk clerk disappears after dropping his name off with me.

My money, cowpoke of the silver screen or starched shirt and silver star, Graves is rich and white and tan all over, not to mention empty inside, like a football with too much hot air in it.

Sheriff Albert Graves made his name starring in Flying A two-reelers like *A Man Comes to Town*, and *Outlaws on the Run*, but when the talkies started squawking and the studio went belly-up, his name stayed on people's lips. He didn't know a statute from a piece of sculpture, but he kissed babies and stood next to politicians like a man born to it, and he won the election in a landslide. He ran on the teetotalers' ticket, but he got reelected with bootleg cash. Everybody won.

I sit under the slow-moving ceiling fan and wait for Graves to come back from wherever it is he went.

After another hour of me counting tiles on the roof next door and losing count halfway through, Graves walks in and pretends to be surprised that I'm here.

He's just like I remember him from the movies, only he talks. Somehow, though, he says less.

He's never heard of Fraley, Sampson, O'Mara, Mars, Calvin Coolidge, Herbert

Hoover, the Pope, Jesus Christ, or Babe Ruth. He's never heard of the mayor, he's a little fuzzy on his wife and kids, and he intends to forget that he met me within the hour. I collect my hat and the package that I checked at the door, and head for the nearest shoeshine stand to see if they can go the sheriff and the directory one better. One better is one, so far.

Funny thing about this town, shoes must stay shined. There isn't a shine box anywhere, or else I keep turning the same two corners. Could be—everything on this one looks strangely familiar to me. At least they change the names on the buildings. Probably just to keep me awake.

I cross the boulevard again and find myself a seat at EATS. It doesn't take long to find one, because every seat's free. A kid walks in a couple of minutes later, and then at least we both have company. He sits at the other end of the diner, though, and doesn't look like the talkative type.

EATS has a nice view of the asphalt, the thin white stripe, and the palm trees growing in the middle of the boulevard. Some genius put the kitchen on the ocean side, and the dining room on the road side. Past the palms is the endless building that is Santa Teresa. A nice place to live, but I wouldn't want to paint there.

After about fifteen minutes, the waitress comes out of the kitchen and hesitates with her pad, deciding whether to ignore me or the kid first. After a few minutes of adjusting her apron and sniffling, she comes over to take my order, or maybe just to pop gum in my ear. She doesn't say anything, just cocks her head a little and leans in, pad in hand. She's eighteen, nineteen maybe, with ringlets and cat's-eye glasses, and a manner like a mental patient on his medication. She smells like she just broke out of the zoo with a deep-fat fryer.

Her name-tag says "Linda." She says nothing. I ask Linda if she knows anyone named Fraley and she nods, drops a menu in front of me, and leaves without taking my order.

I guess the kid eats first.

Another fifteen minutes and she's back with my cup of Java. I ask her again about Fraley.

"Never heard of her. What'll you have?"

"A minute ago, you said you had. Forget her while you were gone? How about Mars? Eddie Mars?"

"Sure, I know Mr. Mars. Ought to. He owns the joint."

"This place?"

"Yeah."

"Great place Mr. Mars has here. Just like the Brown Derby, only without the charm or the atmosphere. You know, I've been looking for a good way to get in on the ground floor of a hopping joint like this. Suppose you tell me how to get in touch with Mr. Mars?"

"You're a queer one, aren't you? What are you snooping around for? Saw you across the road earlier."

"Go on. What could it hurt? I'm trying to do business with the man, and I don't know how to find him."

"Well, you're not going to find out from me. I don't know how to get in touch with Mr. Mars. Never had to. Lash Yeager runs the place for him."

"Yeager? He ever show with another fellow, guy by the name of Puddler?"

"You are a funny one. Puddler's Lash's nickname. You know Lash?"

"No, but if you hum a few bars, I could fake it. Has Mr. Yeager been in today?"

"No, but he don't always come by. He's down in Los Angeles most days lately. Working on something else, I guess.

Listen, Mister, I got other customers. You gonna order or what?"

"Sure thing, Linda. I'll have the steak, bloody, and a baked potato. And don't be shy with the Java, all right?"

She goes off to take the kid's order. She must be doing the cooking, too, because she stays gone a good long time.

When my mouth is as dry as the coffee cup, I get up to look for Linda. I hear a little clicking in one of the back booths, next to the kitchen. She's sitting there with her back to me, working a piece of needlepoint with her hands in her lap.

I'm going to ask her about the steak, but when I get to that last booth, the hands are still working on the lace, but they're not attached to Linda.

They're attached to a woman wearing all black, with a familiar pair of green eyes, and the hourglass figure of a poisonous spider. She stops knitting long enough to motion me to sit down opposite her.

She already knows my name, of course.

"It is Marlowe, right? I have the right dick, right, dick?"

"You've got the advantage over me, Miss . . . ?"

"My name's not important just now, Mr. Marlowe. Sit down, sit down, *please—you're beginning to fold. And besides, you'll make everyone nervous, standing there like a coat rack without a coat."*

"I'm not folding, I just didn't want anyone to get jealous of my excellent posture."

She gives me a look like she might give a particularly fine piece of garbage that the wind blew into her leg.

She holds the glare for a minute and then picks up the needlepoint and says, "Marlowe, did you know that spiders eat their webs overnight? They spend hours building these incredibly intricate patterns, going in and out and over, exhausting themselves, and then, after they've caught a little lunch—even if they haven't—the web starts to go to pieces, and, rather than let it go to waste, they eat it. The whole thing. Then they start all over again. Hard to believe, huh? I've been working on this pattern for over a month now, sewing whenever I can, and every time I get near the end, I end up unwinding it. I don't really know why—it's supposed to be for my husband."

"Must be one hell of a tough guy, to go in for that kind of stuff."

"Oh, but he was, in his way. A brave man. Maybe a stupid man. This

particular pattern is based on a fisherman's net. My husband was a kind of a fisherman, I guess you could say. To be perfectly honest, I don't really know what he did when he was away. We hadn't really been together for all that long before he disappeared. I was making this for his coffin, Mr. Marlowe. The police tell me he's dead. There was a funeral. Something is buried in the cemetery. But you see, I don't think that it is my husband. They wouldn't show me his body; they said I probably wouldn't be able to identify it anyway, what was left of it. How could they be so sure who it was, then? How could they know?"

I didn't know how to answer that, so I didn't try.

Wherever Linda had gone, it seemed like she wasn't coming back. I couldn't see the kid from where we sat, and nobody else came in. We were alone.

I wrote up my notes, and she worked on her piece. The thing was like a ship's wheel, but with smaller wheels set in between where the spokes meet the planks, and even smaller wheels inside of those wheels. I felt dizzy watching her working on it. She didn't look up at me.

That's the last entry, the last page in the notebook, and that's where we would lose Archer altogether, were it not for the fact that Raymond Chandler was careful, or maybe just prepared. He had another man on the scene.

[45]

Chandler's second pair of eyes was a twenty-two-year old brickbat academy graduate who ran away from home but forgot to join the circus. Outside of Chandler's "Marlowe" file, "Ross Macdonald" doesn't seem to have so much as drawn a breath in the Los Angeles River Basin during 1929; the name is just a crepe beard for Chandler's eyes—also known as Owen Taylor, Dan Wallace, and Floyd Thursby—to hide behind. Taylor had been Julian Pascal's assistant at South Basin prior to his gig as a General Sternwood impersonator in San Francisco, but when Chandler turned him back into a pumpkin, he was forced into playing coachman for Chandler. Chandler rode him as hard as Pascal had trotted him: no more Union Square ovals for the Counterfeit Kid.

If that meant tailing Archer, so be it; Owen Taylor wasn't in any position to complain. If not for the fact that he was the only person on the General's staff who had actually laid hands on the falcon, Taylor would have been up the river and around a bend long before Pascal found out he wasn't married to his wife. Chandler seems to have spent a fair amount of his free time following the case covering Taylor's notes in language so dirty it would make Ms. West turn pink, and none of it to Taylor's credit. Chandler thought he had gotten the high-hat from his assistant, but it looks more like he just didn't want to look the truth in the face—a cake job at South Basin wasn't in the cards for him.

Chandler put the boy on Archer the night before Archer's trip to Santa Teresa, the night that Chandler unraveled the thread that was Julian Pascal. At any rate, that's where Taylor's surveillance file starts weaving.

Chandler might have suspected Archer of holding back; it wouldn't have been the first time Chandler's accomplices had, after all. Fool me once, shame on you. Fool me twice, you've got a good thing going. Chandler didn't like playing the fool; he didn't even like going to the theater.

Taylor wasn't much of a seamstress, but apparently he could pin the tail like a Savile Row tailor working a hem. It could be that Archer was wise, and played the kid along like Hamlet played Claudius, but, given the Elsinore Keep that opens up between Taylor's account and Archer's, it doesn't look even odds. Whatever the case, it's worth reproducing Taylor's notes

—minus Chandler's four-letter lexicon—to round out the sharp's own account.

From the Chandler Taylor surveillance file:

February 5

4:47 PM: Marlowe arrives at office (6383 Hollywood) with some sort of package wrapped up in brown paper; about two feet by one foot by one foot, and it looks heavy. He's also carrying a suit and a notebook. The suit he's wearing's a powder blue number that looks like it was two sizes too small before he washed it: he's all sucked in like a private at drill just to keep the buttons sewed on.

Marlowe stops to detail it with the sleepy fellow behind the desk in his building, then he rides up in the elevator.

5:17 PM: Marlowe exits the Security Trust, jumps the streetcar. Gets off at the Hollywood Hotel, crosses Boulevard, enters the Roosevelt Hotel.

6:01 PM: Marlowe exits, walks east on Hollywood. Stops at 6763 Hollywood, "A.G. Geiger Rare Books and DeLuxe Editions," and looks in the window for a nickel. Might have tapped the glass, too—can't tell from this angle. Broad—unbelievable broad—lamps like you wouldn't believe, and a body to go with them—is at the desk in Geiger's. She might have looked up when Marlowe might have tapped the glass. Playing cute, both of them, but only one of them looks the part. Marlowe crosses the Boulevard, enters diner (First Floor, Christie Hotel, 6724 H'wood).

6:20 PM: Broad and her body exit shop, lock up. Marlowe is sitting in a window booth, watching the street for something. Broad crosses Boulevard to diner, enters. She sits across from him, same booth. They don't look like they're doing much talking. She's got some needlepoint with her, starts working it. Eventually, she passes some papers over the table, and Marlowe reads through them.

6:35 PM: I cross to the south side of the Boulevard to get out of the spotlights the *Egyptian* is throwing over here, and stop next door to the diner, in front of a joint called the Wild Piano, 6726 Hollywood. Some joker with an iron fist in his coat pocket knocks me down. The gat makes me think twice about ringing him up for it, though. Getting up, another acrobat tries to send me back to the pavement and I turn around to sock him one. That's when I notice that I've been standing in front of a picture of the broad from Geiger's the whole time, the broad who's sitting across from Marlowe in the diner. Under a couple big gold stars is the name "Betty Fraley: One Night Only." Whatever else she does to pay the rent, she's an entertainer after dark. She could have my two bits.

I lose the two elbow-rubbers in the crowd in front of the *Egyptian*, but meantime Marlowe exits the diner—minus the arm-candy—and starts off in my direction. I ogle the broad in the picture while he passes me by, but just for a second, I catch Marlowe's eyes in the reflection. He isn't looking at me.

He says something I don't catch and crosses the Boulevard.

6:38 PM: I decide to chance it and take a looksee in the diner. Marlowe's right across the Boulevard from me, not fifty yards from where I just was, and the broad's still sitting at the booth, working on her knitting. I can't tell if Marlowe's watching the diner or what. Behind the counter, some cross-eyed Sam in a paper hat gives me the evil eye—at least, he tries to, but with his eyes all crossed up, it looks like he's confused about who he's giving the evil eye to. I order a cup of joe and sit down at the counter.

I can watch Fraley in my spoon's reflection if I turn it just right. Looks like she's working on a baby sweater, but all in black. I have to turn the stool all the way to the side to peep Marlowe across the street, and a breather in coveralls grunts every time I swivel, so I throw three nickels on the counter and move over to the rag rack to watch from there. The one near the top's upside down: *Black Mask Magazine*, it's called. A couple nice-looking dames on the cover, but just mostly cops-and-robbers stuff inside.

6:45 PM: Marlowe's on the move, back to this side of the Boulevard.

6:47 PM: The Fraley dame finishes up her glass of water, exits, and boards the streetcar outside. "This ain't a library," the dumdum behind the counter tells me, and starts to come around the register, but the grunter in the coveralls taps a couple of times like he's in a hurry, and the gorilla goes back into his cage. I give him the razz and step outside.

Because of the crowd in front of me, I can't see Marlowe, but a spotlight hits Geiger's windows opposite, and in the flash after, I see him in the reflection, up ahead, getting ready to cross Las Palmas. I dodge out into the gutter and around the stiffs, and then I catch him over a wave of hats, already to Cherokee. It isn't until the drugstore at Wilcox that I can see his shoes. He waits for the light to turn, then he gets stopped in the intersection by a brown Packard with its door open.

7:00 PM: Lucky I parked near Marlowe's office. I get to my jalopy just in time to watch the Packard turning west on Selma. It turns north on Highland and up into the hills.

7:20 PM: The Packard lost me somewhere around where Camrose turns into Hillcrest turns into Sycamore turns into Fitch . . . I couldn't keep track of where I was anymore, much less the

Packard. Plus, the fellow driving it must have took his training from the Keystone Kops. I park down near where Orchid dead-ends at Franklin, to wait them out. You can only go so far up there, and there's only one way down. You have to come out some time.

7:56 PM: Shadowing's about as interesting as watching grass grow in a dark basement, only you get half as much done. I've seen the same geezer cross the street now three times and I guarantee he's getting more action than me. No Packards.

8:35 PM: The Packard moves through the intersection at Highland and Franklin, headed south on Highland. I've got my headlamps on them before they get to the Boulevard.

8:37 PM: The Packard parks at the Roosevelt and Marlowe and the other man get out and head inside. Something about the other man looks awful familiar, but he's turned toward the building and I don't catch his face. Maybe it's just that he and Marlowe look like they fell out of the same family tree—same height and build, same color hair. Same cut of suit.

8:45 PM: No sign of Marlowe, but the man with the Packard gets into his jalopy and starts it up. A few minutes later, someone—probably Marlowe in different clothes—comes out of the Roosevelt, and jumps in. I follow the jalopy down to Sunset, and then west to the South Basin offices. Just when I'm thinking this is one hell of a coincidence, Mr.

Chandler, you get out of the Packard. All this time, I've been following you. That's when I detail it with you.

Taylor buttons up for a while after his little revelation, maybe feeling a little sheepish about shadowing the hand that feeds him, especially when that hand is waving a gun around and kidnapping his beat. Chandler tried to cross out the last seven lines, but the notes (or what's reprinted above) show through his ink, and his insults are indication enough of what else might be under it. Dangerous stuff to keep in your files. Even more dangerous not to keep it.

[46]

The South Basin Oil Company offices, until they were moved out to the port following General Sternwood's death in 1933, were located at 9801 Sunset, just down the hill from the Sternwood mansion, on part of the original ranch land that Sternwood bought for beads and bluff from the local state representative after the area had been carefully cleared of any remaining Spaniards. Over the hill and through the woods, an old horse trail led through dry canyons, orange groves, and manicured lawn thicker than a Persian carpet and a lot more expensive, from the South Basin offices on Sunset right to the back door of the Sternwood mansion.

Most of the land was useless: useless for drilling, useless for living, useless for farming or grazing, useless for anything but a firebreak. The hill that the mansion stood on, though, was artificially green all the way down the drive, brown land soaked until it sprouted, and then back behind over the rise up to the lawn, line after line of orange trees covered in dust, as far as the eye could see, until the grade changed and slid down a steep dusty hill to the oil fields, where it was black, through and through. Fifty yards from the nearest derrick, a temporary clapboard rig that the original drillers had used for a canteen had sprouted wings and ells and turned into the Sunset office of the South Basin Oil Company.

The Company was mostly charged with keeping the General's affairs in order: greasing the palms of everyone from Harry Chandler and Buron Fitts down to Louella Parsons and the beat cops walking the streets of West Hollywood. But when it's such sticky business, it's easy to get a little glue on your hands. Most of the board-room boys at South Basin, Pascal included, had found their palms still a little green after they had made their hand-offs, and Chandler made it his mission to turn the spade on their soil. When General Sternwood arrived at the 1929 Christmas party in his Santa costume, ready for the secretaries to tell him whether they'd been naughty or nice and not caring either way, Chandler was one of only three employees there who had been at the 1928 party, and the other two were sitting on Santa's lap. He stuck with what he knew, asset-recovery, following the money. In a place like South Basin that could only put you in one of two places: the boardroom or jail. By the time Pascal's corner offices were cleaned out, Chandler was Vice-President, and in a good position to see many more South Basin Christmas parties, so long as he could keep the dirt from settling on him.

The particular dirt that Chandler and South Basin were charged with cleaning up at the time of Chandler's promotion was plastered all over the front pages: "Local Businessman Missing!" ran the February 6, 1929 *Times*, above the fold in block type as big as it comes. Evidently, someone wasn't doing their job: the reason for the fanfare was Ralph Sampson, a man who owned nearly as much of the Southland as the General, and who had last been seen leaving Santa Teresa to catch the Santa Monica-bound ferry at Goleta the morning of February 5, on his way to visit the offices of South Basin Oil. The best Chandler had been able to do was to keep the reason for his visit out of the papers, but what if it had been related to the errand that Chandler sent Archer on that night? What if Sampson's disappearance had less to do with a drunken chauffeur on the coast road than a falcon flapping in the wind? Some coincidences are just coincidences, but most aren't.

[47]

Owen Taylor slipped out of Chandler's files overnight, as thin as the air between two sheets of paper, but he was back in black and white the next morning, all got up in chauffeur's livery, waiting on Archer at the Ivar office. Taylor was sitting behind the wheel of the General's borrowed Rolls Royce Phantom landau, but Archer was going to be doing the steering.

7:22 AM: Marlowe exits office, climbs into blue Ford coupe. Stops off at the diner at the Christie for a plate of hash and a cup of joe. The never-blinks is still behind the counter, so I don't chance it. I just wait outside in the car, bump on a log.

7:45 AM: Marlowe back in blue Ford. South on Highland, then west on Santa Monica all the way until Los Angeles runs out of land to pave.

9:35 AM: After a whole lot of waiting and a close call with a prowl car, Marlowe boards the Goleta ferry. The prowler does too. I'm last on, or, at least, there aren't any other takers this morning.

While Marlowe is trying to reel some flying fish in with his stare, I sneak out of the Rolls and up to the cabin. The captain doesn't like me any more than he does the copper on the deck, but a flash of silver and a nip from the flask in my jacket pocket convince him otherwise.

He tells me that Goleta is a feed store, two restaurants, and a ferry terminal shy of being sand and rocks. The action, he says, is down the coast road to where it dead-ends, a town called Santa Teresa, where you can get anything you want if you've got the right name and the right door. He gives me an address and tells me that the open-sesame is "Eddie sent me." I ask him if he's Eddie and he gives me a look like I just dropped a bag of hammers on my own foot and then kicked it.

"You need to get wise, kid, or you'll wind up six feet under with a whole lot of mud on top. Maybe Santa Teresa's not your speed. You don't know who Eddie is, you shouldn't be attending his garden party, you get my drift?"

"Sure thing, Pops. Sure thing."

I blow him a razz and climb back into the Rolls while Marlowe's still checking his line.

After we dock, Marlowe zips south on the coast road. There's no traffic to cover me, but according to the tin-whistler on the ferry, there's only one destination down south anyway: Santa Teresa, Eddie's town. I cool my heels in Goleta at a restaurant called Tom's, a big empty place with eggs like salted, cured rubber and coffee that you can drink with a knife and fork.

11:04 AM: Santa Teresa must be a real late-night kind of burg: everybody's still asleep when I roll in. Nobody on the streets anywhere, not in a car, not on a bicycle, not on a horse, not on foot: not a single solitary person to ruin the view. Not much of a view, either; you can't see the ocean because some genius decided to make all the buildings facing the other way, towards the mountains. But you can't see them either; all you can really see is the next white stucco building, because they're all exactly the same height.

I had one hell of a time figuring out how to get the Rolls into town. I spotted the blue Ford back on the coast road, parked at some joint called EATS, but luckily Marlowe wasn't around to make me. I got to say, I don't know why you wanted me to take the Rolls, Mr. Chandler—it's like wearing a sunflower in your lapel and a pink stovepipe hat. Even a sucker would spot a tail driving the landau. Best I can do is pretend General Sternwood's in back, we're out for a Sunday drive. Only it ain't Sunday.

There's a little turn after the EATS place, and the sheriff's office is just around the corner. I figure there won't be a safer place to leave the Rolls, so I park it there and hoof it the rest of the way.

11:37 AM: I make Marlowe snooping around outside the sheriff's. He's carrying the brown paper package from before. He keeps shifting it from one hand to the other.

The streets here just stop on a dime, all one-way turns and dead-ends, so I have to keep it slow, not get too close. It's like crawling through sand in a hurry. I take the cornerstones easy because there's no cover and barely any noise to cover my steps. Marlowe's acting like he knows where he's going, but in the end, all he finds is the sheriff's again. We're back where we started.

12:16 PM: Whatever Marlowe was looking for stayed invisible, I guess. He starts heading off in the direction he took me in first, but then angles off through a back alley to the coast road, and crosses over to EATS. I think about going back for the Rolls, in case he's moving on, but I can't figure how we got here. Right through the first little plaza, but then there are a couple of turns that could go either way. I step out onto the coast road to go around the couple of blocks to where I parked the Rolls that way, but it turns out he's just going for some grub.

I decide to get some coffee in me, keep an eye on him. I pull the hat down, cross the boulevard, and step in to the diner.

The dame from last night, Fraley, is in a back booth, next to the kitchen, with her sewing basket, working on whatever it was she was working on last night. Marlowe's sitting across from her, his brown-paper package on the table between them.

1:35 PM: Marlowe and Fraley jawed pretty steadily for half an hour. I sipped my coffee real slow. When I ran out of coffee, I ordered a second lunch, steak and potatoes, then I pushed it around my plate while Marlowe and the dame stared at each other. After another two bits or so, the Fraley dame took the package and scrammed, leaving her knitting behind. Marlowe waited a few beats, picked up the basket, and went to the washroom.

When he came out, he was wearing a different suit, a bright green number, like he just landed a job guarding a pot of gold. When he passed, I noticed there wasn't any knitting in the basket, like I had thought; there was a big lump underneath a black blanket. I didn't want to look like I was interested, so I didn't get a good squint.

Marlowe got in his jalopy and headed north and I hurried across the boulevard to the Rolls. The Santa Monica-bound ferry was leaving at 2:15; he'd really have to lay tracks to make it. I pushed the Rolls up to red line.

4:05 PM: Marlowe pulls out of the service station onto Santa Monica Boulevard, with company. A gray Ford coupe just like his picked him up getting off the ferry, two bruisers in the front seat.

They give him just enough space to let him know what they're up to, and he tries to lose them.

4:21 PM: The coupes handle a little better than the Rolls; I lose the caravan and stop on the side of the boulevard, hope they're on their way back into town.

4:32 PM: The gray Ford coupe pulls out in front of me, with Marlowe in his leprechaun outfit stuffed between the two heavies like the cheese in a tramp's sandwich. I follow, as far back as I can manage. Don't want to spook these guys; the car's full. I'd end up in the trunk.

4:57 PM: The gray Ford coupe pulls up at the office. How is it we always end up here? The bruisers manhandle Marlowe out of the jumpseat, around the office to the fields.

Marlowe tries a break after they pass the derricks, but one of the giants wrestles him to the ground. They both end up with tar on them. The two walking volcanoes pull out a couple of heaters and wave them at Marlowe. He takes the hint and starts up the hill in front of them.

About thirty minutes and maybe two and a half miles uphill in the hot sun, we're in the orange grove and I'm sweating enough to water a whole line of trees.

The two goons start one way through the grove with Marlowe, then turn around. They look a little confused, a lot stupid. I have to fade way back into the first row so that they don't make me.

Now they start off in my direction. They don't get twelve steps toward me before Marlowe breaks free again and dodges through a line of trees. The trees here are so close together that you can barely see the light coming through them, and the goons lose him in there before they can put iron on him.

Only way I can track him is at the ankle, that green suit against the gray-brown of the orange trees. Above the ankles, he blends into the green like a lizard on a leaf, unless he's on the move. The two goons are more like spiders on white bread, with their dark pinstripes. You could pick them out in the gaps or down the row easy as apples and oranges. They circle him, but every time they break through a row, he's a ghost.

The pickers move from row to row through these gaps in the rows, gaps that must eventually lead you to the center of the grove to where the well is, or out from the center to the wheelbarrows, but the gaps aren't spaced regular or anything, you just come up on them from out of nowhere. I lay back in one, between the third and fourth rows, and I see Marlowe about forty yards down the row where the grove's bend is. The tar on his green suit is collecting dust and turning the thing brown, ankles up. He's stopped, too, peeping through the next gap, maybe trying to clear it before stepping through.

It's hot out here, and dry as a slice of toast. The five o'clock sun might as well be ten feet away and right overhead. So still you can hear somebody else's heart beating.

Back on the first or second row, the two heavies are grousing to each other. To put a little distance between us, I head down to where Marlowe stopped; he's already long gone. But while I'm standing there, trying to decide my next move, smelling that breakfast rolled in dirt smell that the trees have, I notice that the dust is cleaned off of the leaves at the right side of the closest gap, like somebody just brushed up against them. I could follow him by watching the leaves on the gaps.

I push through into the next row, but I don't see anybody. Then I notice a puff of dust coming up to the right. Marlowe.

I follow his gusts through a couple more gaps, but I never catch sight of him. I figure by now, we must be pretty close to the well, but since it's just trees, there's no way to really tell until we get to the clearing. If we had already gone past it, it would look like this, too, I guess.

I hang my coat on a branch next to me and peel off an orange. If it ain't cold, at least it's wet. There's a rustling. Black shows through under the leaves—the heavies for sure. I duck back through the last gap and get about fifty yards down that row, looking for the next one to put a little air between me and their ventilators. That's when I realize that I left my coat back there on the branch. It's always the details.

About another forty paces down, there's another gap back into the row I was just on. I slip into the gap and hold my breath. Nothing. A bee buzzes my face real close and settles on the Colorado of sweat coming down out of my hat, next to my ear. I'm doing my best statue and hoping the sonofabitch bee will am-scray. No dice. I swat at it. The damn thing stings me. I yelp and slap my cheek where it landed.

Lucky for me, the yelp and the slap are covered up by the unbelievably loud sound of a hand cannon going off. Lucky for me. Not so lucky for somebody else. I wipe the bee off on my pants and check down the row where I left my coat. Nothing. I creep down the row to the gap where I left it. No soap. No coat either. I can see where it was: there's clean branches there, no coat. One of the goons must have took it. Not that either one of them could fit into it with a shoehorn and a paint bucket full of grease.

Whoever it is, they've got my wallet. Maybe they haven't checked the pockets yet. But I only got the "Ross Macdonald" card in there, so they'll be on the wrong track before they even start looking anyway. I check the dirt for shoe prints and follow the pair that isn't mine up to a gap farther on.

When I get to the next bend, I spot someone in a pinstripe up ahead. Only it's not one of the gorillas from the coupe—these stripes are wider than a pin. They're wider than a pencil, even. He's facing the opposite way from me, so I keep on up the row until I can get to the next gap and some cover. That's when some fellow ducks out of one of the rows ahead, about halfway between this new fellow and me. This new fellow's not even wearing his jacket, just carrying it. I would say he's a smart guy, but the dope's not wearing a hat, either. He goes through a gap into the next row and I lose track of him, trying to keep the fellow in the wide-stripe in my line of sight.

When I get up to the gap that this new gee jumped out of, there's an ugly brown coat with a queer texture hanging there. It's got some tar on the front. Marlowe's coat. There's nothing in the pockets except a fake detective license that says Philip Marlowe.

My size, though. I turn around and take off down the row, trying to get a bead on the hatless fellow's ankles. Nothing.

One of the goons from the coupe is up ahead, peeking in to the next row, with a gat in his off hand. Closer I get, though, I notice it isn't one of the goons from the coupe after all. Whoever it is, he's got on a black suit, could be my jacket. I'm just about to ask him when there's a shot from the next row over, and he ducks through the gap like a cat that doesn't want to be picked up.

That's where Macdonald's notes—and Macdonald himself—end. Taylor, too, seems to have disappeared. South Basin cuts just two more checks to him, but there's no way to tell if he cashed either one. No one reports him missing or anything that dramatic, it's just that no one reports anything on him—not then, not ever. Like a magician's mistake, Taylor is thin air from that day forward. Likewise Archer.

[48]

The *Obituaries* column in the Sunday, February 10, 1929 *Times* has its share of worm-food, but none of the stiffs fits the description of Archer—or Taylor for that matter. What can I say: some people never make the papers. If Archer had gone the way of the dodo, there wouldn't have been an ornithologist to mark his passing anyway.

Marvin Smith, 44, beloved husband and father of 7, died in an automobile accident at the intersection of Hollywood and Vine. Funeral February 14, at Calvary Cemetery.

William Gumphrey, 41, beloved son, died of natural causes. He will be remembered by his mother and his stepfather, Mr. and Mrs. Alfred Mansfield.

Jonathon Frisk, 39, father of two (no cause of death, must have been a bad one). Any information on next of kin can be sent care of

Hollygrove, Orphan's Home Society, Los Angeles, California.

Benjamin C. Hawley, 41, died at brother's home while visiting Hollywood from Concord, Massachusetts. Services will be held in Concord.

Frederick "Moose" Lovell, 45, Southern Pacific employee, died of injuries suffered during switching yard accident. He will be remembered by his three sons and his daughter.

Joseph Morganroth, 49, IN MEMORIAM: "In loving memory of my husband, our father," by wife and children.

[49]

On May 6, 1933, General Norris Sternwood finally sealed the deal on that farm he always wanted. The notice in the *Times* doesn't give out the circumstances of his passing. He was survived by his two daughters, Vivian and Carmen Sternwood, who took the money and ran. It's never far enough or fast enough.

Vivian Sternwood married a Mr. William Wilson, of Chicago, Illinois on August 12, 1933, in Santa Teresa. Mr. Wilson took his new bride home to Chicago, where he worked at publishing some sort of scandal sheet. He also did all of the reporting on it. The two apparently lived in matrimonial harmony for almost five years, when, in January of 1939, Wilson was apparently run down by a streetcar and his body—rendered unrecognizable by the accident—was buried in the Sternwood plot in Forest Lawn. Vivian moved back in to the family home, where she lived, alone except for the bats in the belfry, until her death in 1962.

Her sister, Carmen, tied the knot, too—there's a notice in the *Times* gossip section for May 16, 1934—but the paperwork seems to have gone missing from city files, and the blurb in the *Times* doesn't list the dipstick's name. Whatever other adventures the two had, she was playing deaf, dumb, and blind in the Hopwood Nursing Home of La Jolla, California by 1938, listed as "incurable," in a "vegetative state." No word on whether she was the peas or the carrots. She passed away in her sleep on August 9, 1945, just minutes after "Fat Man" flattened the city of Nagasaki. Visitation records from the home list just one visitor in the last year, a "Philip Marlowe," who visited six times between July and August of that year, and may have been present at the time of Carmen's death.

Ralph Sampson played the bad penny and never turned up. After almost two years of wrangling with the insurance boys to have her father declared dead, Penelope Sampson became the richest woman in California. All that money bought her the boxcarload of privacy she always wanted; after signing the papers on the settlement, she never again saw her name in print. She learned something from the old man after all.

In the fall of 1933, a few months after the General shuffled off this mortal coil, the catalog from the Sternwood estate auction lists "One black statuette, 24x12x10, unidentified stone, subject: bird in profile. Excellent condition: wear marks at base and around eyes, some chipping. Believed to be of Italian or Greek make." The buyer is not reported.

Raymond Chandler's 1933 was spent unemployed and holed up in his study and in various seedy hotels up and down the Southern California coast. The General had bounced him like a bad check, and made sure he had no future in oil in the Southland. Even the Lloyds turned up their noses at him. Chandler spent his summer, fall, and winter vacation reading the pulps, scooping out their plots like digging out a pumpkin to make a Jack-O-Lantern, and then trying to get the seeds to grow into full-fledged stories again. Sometimes it worked, mostly it didn't. That didn't keep him from trying. His black thumb eventually turned green with a Blue Ribbon crop, watering his rows by changing the no-name heroes of his stale stories to "Philip Marlowe." He had discovered "write what you know" late in life.

In the spring of 1933, Dashiell Hammett published what would be his final novel, *The Thin Man*, at Alfred A. Knopf. It had been a very brief career, but he traded on it for the rest of his natural life. He kept stringing his publishers along, telling them that he was working on the follow-up, but for his last three decades, all he was really doing was banging a mostly empty head against an awfully thick wall. He moved down to Los Angeles in the summer of 1933 to try to make some money in the movie business, but couldn't even manage that. He wrote a letter to his wife, the first in a year, asking her to join him there, and then, when she had, moved, without her, to New York. He couldn't be tied down. Say what you want about the man, at least he was consistently inconsistent.

Kenneth Millar, the boy who was celebrated in the July 7, 1928 edition of the *Los Gatos Mail*, would claim that he saw his father alive in the fall of 1939, in the Queen Elizabeth Hospital for Incurables, in Toronto. The fact that Jack Millar had been declared dead nearly ten years earlier hadn't ended the man's life, just his good health: Jack Millar couldn't speak, his son later reported, but he could write messages on a small chalkboard kept by his bedside especially for the purpose. Most of them were completely illegible, even to the nurses; the one identifying the man as Kenneth's father was the only one that anyone could read.

EDITOR'S NOTE

About three months after the publication of "The Little Death," the fruit of my year-long investigation into the events that Raymond Chandler fictionalized in his novel *The Big Sleep*, I received a brown-paper wrapped, phone-book sized package in the mail. It was much heavier than a phone book, I thought, denser—broader, too. When the carrier handed it to me, I could barely hold it up against my side with my left hand as I signed for it with my right. I set it down on the side table with a ringing thump that brought the attention of my fiancée, Jessica. There was no return address anywhere on the paper, and she asked me how it had been delivered in the first place: "I thought there had to be a return address," she said, examining it at arm's length. I guessed not.

My first thought was that someone had sent me a bomb, possibly someone from the Greene estate, unhappy with the portrait I had painted of

Helga and her father in the essay, or, for that matter, the particular shape I had invented for Mr. Chandler, for whom I had nothing but the greatest respect for as a writer but who had come off as bungling and hapless in my recounting of the events of his life. I briefly considered calling the police, but thankfully, thought better before I embarrassed myself, exposing my hubris. I was, after all, no one. No one would want me dead.

I was relieved and somewhat puzzled, then, when I lugged the package to my study's desk, unwrapped the old-fashioned butcher paper tied with string, and found a kind of black laquered Chinese box with this manuscript inside, along with reams of photocopied pages from a journal, a few poorly photocopied photographs, and a letter from the author.

The photographs were evidently already aged and damaged when the author found them. The photocopies he made of those photographs are further darkened and damaged, and our attempts to reproduce them here resulted in rather dim, completely uninterpretable pictures, silhouettes and vague backgrounds that would have thrown no light whatsoever on the proceedings. Our profuse apologies to any disappointed readers and, of course, to the author, for the decision not to include them in the present edition.

Here is the letter, in its entirety:

Dear Mr. Blackwell,

You might be riding a high horse now, but still you're all wet. Stanley Reilly was a bit player, a placeholder, a zero. The gee you're after went by the name of Lewis Miles Archer and I can prove it.

When Raymond Chandler died in 1959, his executor called me in to look over his papers. It took some legwork, the better part of a decade, and more than a little calabash, but I managed to pick up the bread crumbs Chandler had left behind there. Deep in the heart of the forest, Archer's notebook and a black bird were waiting. Chandler didn't get his hands on it, but I did. This is the real play, with the main characters on stage, not behind the curtain where you had them.

The scribbles in the photocopies I've sent are in Archer's handwriting; shorthand that kept getting longer every time I went at it. It took me a couple of years just to break the code, and even then, I probably lost a few important characters here and there. That's life. The other pages are from Chandler's private correspondence and from his files at South Basin. There should be enough there to convince you I'm not trying to put anything over on you. You want to try to go into it more, that's your look-out.

The photographs aren't the ones that Chandler and Archer jawed about. Those never turned up. I found most of these in Chandler's files from the South Basin days (somehow they got moved along with the potted plants and double-entry ledgers to the port office when South Basin closed the Sunset office in 1933), but they had been handled more often than a lever on a San Francisco streetcar. The rest are from a roll of film that went to a shop on Hollywood Boulevard named Spanner Camera, a place that Archer mentions in his notebook; I circled that part for you. Spanner was shuttered long before I got to their name in the notebook, but a bit of sleuthing and a show of the long green got me the few snaps that hadn't been too badly overexposed by Archer's overexposure. The lady that you see sitting on the throne in the altogether is Iva Goodbody, a.k.a. Iva Archer, a.k.a. Penelope Sampson. I've included some pictures of Ms. Goodbody from her Ziegfeld days, just in case you think I'm passing bad bills. Same dame.

The trail on Archer is Antarctica. Colder than cold. Nothing anyone can do about it now. My advice: don't bother trying to go too much further down that road. It's a dead-end.

Listen, Blackwell, I'm not the egghead—you are. Anyway I'm tired of this story. It's yours now. If you have to change the names around a little bit, I won't grumble. A two-faced group like this is asking for it anyway. Just make sure you get the facts straight. Chandler was on to something when he said that the only good kinds of mysteries are the ones where you can follow along with the detective. All the rest of it is fantasy, Aesop without the animals. There aren't any morals in real life, just a whole lot of work and plenty of dying.

The letter was unsigned.

My investigation of the previous year had taken all of my savings and a great deal of time on the road, away from home. Those travels had occasioned the loss of my position; my job was not one that provided for time off, and I was let go after my first trip to Los Angeles. My relationship with Jessica was strained: she had been able to accompany me on only one of my trips, and was beginning to suspect that something besides research was being done on these frequent and often unplanned journeys. Nonetheless, she had done the difficult work of paying the rent on our apartment without my help, asking only for time together when I happened to be home. Because of my wholly justified fear that, should the investigation stretch any further than it already had, I might attract the unwanted attentions of the Greene estate and find myself the defendant in a libel suit—nullifying the work I had already done and possibly ending my career before it had even begun—I could not even give her that, for which I sincerely repented.

With the essay written and those trials over, I had been hoping to find a position in town, to fit back into my former life with Jessica in Portland, as though the cards had merely been reshuffled rather than having endured a round of 52 pickup. Just after I had received the package and before I had begun my fact-checking and code-breaking, and with the prospects of some sort of gainful employment and a normal social life still dangling enticingly in front of me, Jessica knocked at the door of my study—a long, narrow hallway that led to a blocked-off door that I had outfitted with a desk and a set of shelves—and brought me what would have been, in any other but our present circumstances, joyous news. She was pregnant.

Our bank account was as hollow as an empty cupboard, and, when I knocked, so were my job prospects. Jessica's health had begun to falter under the continual strain of providing for two people on her pittance, and we both stared, shocked, at our future together and the child that we, it seemed, would bring into it. How could we pay for childcare when we couldn't afford insurance or car payments? How could we care for it when we were doing so poorly with ourselves? How could we even afford to feed it when our pantry stayed empty for weeks at a time?

Throughout, she resisted calling it "it." "The baby," she insisted, over and over. For my own part, I spoke little on the subject but could think of little else. I did not see a little boy or a little girl. I saw struggle. I saw fear. I had hoped to find, somewhere inside, instead, determination, steel. We avoided talking about it; we began to avoid each other.

I tried even harder to find a career for myself, willing a decision to come. I had been, up until then, a student, supporting myself by waiting tables on weekends and occasionally tutoring high school students. Expenses were minimal, and I worked my hardest at keeping them that way, to allow me time in my study with the door closed, doing research and writing, things that would never lead to financial security except incidentally. But now school was out, my waiting job long gone, my writing no longer an excuse with the essay's publication. I couldn't, I considered, have supported three on a weekend of tips and three hours of physics, composition, and advanced mathematics anyway.

But nothing came and still nothing came. My letters of application fell on deaf ears. My resume was sculpted, sanded, and polished, then painted and repolished, until I no longer recognized myself in it. And while waiting for something—anything—I mined that huge pile of notebook, manuscript, file, and letters.

I had nowhere left to go; I picked up the anonymous writer's trail. I felt certain that I was helping, in my own small way, to blaze a pathway to the truth. Always, the truth. I began an index to the manuscript [the finished version of which is included in this edition]. I found and corrected small errors, most often of clarity or continuity, but also sometimes of the few facts that I could verify on my own [those errors have been silently corrected in this edition], through my previous research and the little I was able to do from Portland.

All through my public job hunt and its private reciprocal, Jessica agonized with her own decisions. Still we did not talk about it, prepared our small talk well ahead of time and carried it out in those rare hours we were both home and I was not in the study, she was not with her friends. I felt guilty. I do not know what she felt; she would not tell me and I could not ask. Any mention of the thing that was coming devolved into argument. Should she get rid of it? The phrasing was all wrong: this was not an it, this was a child; one could not rid oneself of something that was a part of one. I felt her phrasing gave too much weight to one particular outcome and told her so. On this, we did not argue. Even as I recognized that my need to establish the verity of the facts in that brown paper package was rending the delicate fabric of my life with Jessica, still I was unable to curb that desire with any other than discovery, investigation. I had, after all, already very nearly destroyed my life for what this brick through the window was claiming was nothing more than yet another slick fiction—and, worse, it was being proven right at every turn. I was, or had been, all wet after all.

Jessica's morning sickness advanced quickly, and it would soon become impossible to hide her state from the people that she worked with. The time for a decision had come. We agreed on what to do only when it was not being discussed.

Thorny problems assaulted me from all angles: the Archer code, I was certain, was almost broken—some passages, I thought, now came clear, while others remained opaque. I was on the verge of cracking it. I was certain. Only a few more days, I promised her. The truth would out. I told her my prospects looked good. I did not tell her that the word did not refer to a career—at least, not a remunerative one.

My dreams most nights kept me running in circles, and I often awoke ready only for several cups of coffee followed quickly by a rather prolonged nap. When Jessica returned home from work late in the afternoons, I was only just getting up from my nap and starting in to work. Weeks passed when we saw each other not even in dreams, as her schedule changed and my own grew increasingly erratic.

One night, though, nearing the point of no return where our decision was concerned, my sleep was blissfully unclouded by nightmare, and I awoke the next morning with the startling realization that I had it: I had the key to Archer's code. I set to work immediately. Real progress, pages and pages. The manuscript was the true account, my own, earlier accounting a shrewd fraud, yet another fiction, but it did not matter. I had it. Though this progress proved beyond a doubt that the past year had been as nothing, still I couldn't wait to share the revelation with my love. When the time for her to be home had come and gone, I got up from my desk, leaving a weighty stack of decoded and transcribed pages, and wandered around the apartment, calling her name. It was distressingly empty. The shadows lay deeper on every surface, the slanted light did not reach as far. My steps sounded louder. Where could she be?

On the small, round table in the kitchen was a note. Out of respect to her, I do not reprint it here. She had gone. Her clothes and her few possessions had been shuttled away some time or times in the past weeks and I, locked away in my study, had not even noticed. The furniture, the housewares, the television, those things that we had bought together, as well as anything I might be likely to remark in its absence, had been left in place. The apartment was a picture of my life before her, with these phantom accounts of our years together like so many paper dolls glued into scissored snapshots, as though her part in my life had been nothing more than a figment of my imagination. It was as though she had never existed, but still the years had passed, life, accomplished.

I sat down at the table and read over the note again. The words had not changed. I found some comfort in this. What else could I do at that moment? Eventually, I had to put it aside. Work, the desk, *Archer*: what else was there?

INDEX

280 INDEX

Abbott, William (Bud), 222

A. G. Geiger, Rare Books and DeLuxe Editions (for proprietor, *also see* Geiger, Arthur Gwynn), 127, 160, 182-183, 240-241, 243

Albert Samuels Jewelers, 91

Alexander III of Macedon (Alexander the Great), 227

Alice in Wonderland, 131

A Man Comes to Town (film), 230

American Film Manufacturing Company (*also see* Flying A Studio), 218, 230

Archer Investigations, 13-14, 19-22, 26-27, 38, 43, 46-49, 51, 62, 79-80

Archer, Iva (*also see* Goodbody, Iva, *also see* Sampson, Penelope), 23-25, 78, 87, 90-91, 149, 206, 224, 263, 272

    wedding, 24-25

Archer, Lewis Miles, 11-15, 18-28, 38, 41, 46-57, 59, 62-78, 81, 85, 87, 89-91, 93-151, 154-169, 175-185, 187-199, 201-202, 210-217, 226-237, 239, 249, 259, 271-272

    birth, 11-12

    wedding, 24-25

Archer, Miles (character in *The Maltese Falcon*), 28-29, 78, 87

Ares, Theodoro, 85

Argonauts, 15

Bank of America and Italy, 47, 49-51, 57-58, 61-62, 84

Bank of British North America (*also see* Bank of Montreal), 45

Bank of Montreal (*also see* Bank of British North America), 45

Bank of San Francisco, 104

Barbary Coast (*see* San Francisco, California)

Batzel, Larry, 128-130, 140-141, 147, 185, 187-190

Beale, Caroline, 47

Beale, George, 47, 50, 65-68

Beery, Wallace, 184

Biederbecke, Bix, 128

Black Mask Magazine, 70, 242

Bloody Thursday (dockworkers' strike), 50

Bodie, California, 126

Boston Red Sox (baseball team), 12

Bowen, Goodridge (*also see* Pascal, Julian), 44, 170, 191

British Army, 128

Brody, Carmen, 93-96, 105-107

Brody, Joe, 93-98, 100, 105-107, 109-110, 113, 116-118, 122, 150, 154, 169-170

Bronson Cave, 106

Brooklyn Dodgers (baseball team), 12

Brown Derby (restaurant), 233

Cairo, Joel, 59, 88, 203

California State Penitentiary at San Quentin, 110

Capone, Alphonse Gabriel (Al), 113, 128

Carmady, Ted, 92-93, 105, 143-146, 149, 154, 169, 174-180, 189

Catalina Island, California, 140

Chandler, Cissy (*also see* Hurlburt, Pearl Eugenie, *also see* Pascal, Cissy), 44, 173-177, 192

    wedding, 44, 192

Chandler, Harry, 152, 184, 247

Chandler, Raymond Thornton, 12, 28, 43-47, 49-51, 56, 80-81, 86-87, 173-174, 177-180, 190-199, 201-204, 207-216, 237-239, 245, 247-248, 264, 269-272

    birth, 12

    wedding, 44, 192

Chaplin, Charles (Charlie), 107

Charles V of Spain (Holy Roman Emperor), 83

Chicago, Illinois, 12, 16, 27, 60, 262

Chicago White Sox (baseball team), 12

    Comiskey Park, 216

Chinese Theatre, 184

Christ, Jesus, 231

Christie Hotel (*see* Hotel Christie)

Cleveland, Grover, 129
Cocoanut Grove (restaurant), 125
Collins, Peter, 25
Collinson, William (Judge), 25
Colossus of Rhodes, 148
Comiskey Park (*see* Chicago White Sox)
Coney Island (*see* New York, New York)
Constantinople, Turkey, 206
Coolidge, Calvin, 12, 231
Costello, Lou, 222
Crete, 206
    Heraklion (city), 206
Crocker Langly San Francisco Directory, 25
Cyclone (rollercoaster), 194
The Cypress Club (restaurant), 128, 139-140, 142, 147, 202-204, 213, 224
Dalmas, Claudine, 32-37
Dalmas, John, 32-37
Dalmas, John, Jr., 34
Daly, Carroll John, 185
Davenport Hotel (Spokane, Washington), 34
Debs, Eugene V., 12
Delilah's (brothel), 223
de Sade (*see* Francois, Donatien Alphonse)
de Young Museum (San Francisco), 159
Dundy, Barton Maclane, 68
Diner (*see* Hotel Christie)
Earhart, Amelia, 12
Edison, Thomas Alva, 171
Egyptian Theatre, 131, 187, 241-242
El Capitan Theater, 182
Elks Club (organization), 36
Esau, 152
Estabrook, Fay, 35, 223-224
"Fat Man" (atomic bomb), 263
Fitts, Buron, 110, 247
Fleming, Victor, 203
Flitcraft, (?), 29-32
Flying A Studio 218, 230

The Flying Dutchman, 138
Forest Lawn (cemetery in Los Angeles, California), 262
Fort Knox, 205
Fraley, Elizabeth (Betty), 204, 209-214, 241-243, 253
Francois, Donatien Alphonse, 123
Franklin, Benjamin, 48
Gatsby, Jay, 24
Geiger, Arthur Gwynn, 130, 149
Goodbody, Iva (*also see* Archer, Iva, *also see* Sampson, Penelope), 23-25, 272
Good Housekeeping, 23
Gold Rush, 15
Goleta, California, 24, 220, 226, 248, 250-251
Goleta-Santa Monica ferry, 129-131, 139, 165, 213, 220, 226, 248, 251-254
Graves, Albert, 230
Greeley, Horace, 24
Gutman, Caspar, 84-85, 87-88
Hamlet (play written by Shakespeare), 144
Hammett, Josephine Dolan (Jose), 17-19, 24, 27
Hammett, Richard (Dick), 16
Hammett, Samuel Dashiell, 12-24, 26-39, 41, 43, 46-47, 49-51, 56-57, 59-64, 70-71, 78-79, 81-85, 87-88, 90-91, 264
    birth, 12
Hammettville, Maryland, 16
Harold Hardwicke Steiner, Rare Books and DeLuxe Editions, 96-101, 108-109, 111, 115-117, 125-127, 130, 144-145, 147-148, 166, 174, 176, 179, 203
Hellman, Lillian, 27
Hemingway, Ernest, 28
Hercules, 131
Hobart Arms, 108
Hollywood Boulevard, 92, 95, 98-101, 107-110, 117, 127, 131-132, 136-138, 144, 148, 157, 175-176, 183-184, 187-188, 194, 203, 209, 215, 217-218, 240-244, 272

Hollywood, California, 94, 97, 117, 147, 153-154, 171, 173, 188, 194, 218, 247, 261
Hollywood Hotel (see Hotel Hollywood)
Holmes, Sherlock, 175
Hong Kong, 36, 58-59, 85
Hoover, Herbert, 231
Hotel Christie (Hollywood, California), 129, 184, 191, 241, 249
    Diner (1st floor), 98, 100, 108, 129-132, 182-186, 241-242, 249
Hotel Hollywood, 135, 240
Hotel Roosevelt (see Roosevelt Hotel)
Hotel St. Francis (San Francisco, California), 57-59, 70-73, 77, 81, 203
Hoyle, Edmond (1672-1769), 176
Huck, Arthur G., 34-36
Humpty Dumpty (fictional character), 168
Hunter-Dulin Building (Los Angeles, California), 13
Hurlburt, Pearl Eugenie, 24, 44
Illinois (state), 128, 222
Inglewood, California, 185
Iowa (state), 139
Iowa City, Iowa, 132
Ireland (country), 34
Isthmus of Panama, 15
Jacob, 152
Jezebel (ship), 36
John's (restaurant), 67
Jolson, Al, 12
Kansas (state), 132
Keystone Kops, 243
Kitchener (city in Ontario Province, Canada), 12
Knights of Malta, 83
Knopf, Alfred A., 22, 29-30, 264
KNX (Los Angeles-area radio station), 185
Lake Michigan, 11
La Jolla, California, 263
La Paloma (ship), 36, 54, 59

L. D. Walgreen's Family Insurance Company (*also see* Walgreen, L. D.), 13
Lights of New York (film), 12
Lindbergh, Charles, 12
Lindy hop (dance style), 125
Li, Xu, 53-55, 85
Lloyd, Alma, 45, 71, 264
Lloyd, Warren, 45, 71, 264
Los Angeles, California, 17, 27, 36, 39, 44-45, 51, 71, 80, 86, 91, 104, 110, 170-173, 184, 202-203, 205-206, 218, 227, 233, 238, 249, 261, 265
    Fish Harbor (area of), 129
    Skid Road (area of), 157
Los Angeles Express, 110, 205
Los Angeles Times, 110, 185, 205, 248, 260, 262-263
Los Angeles Creamery, 45
Los Gatos, California, 40-41, 62, 73
Los Gatos Mail, 38, 42, 78, 265
Lozelle, Agnes, 148, 160-162, 169
Lucian of Samosata, 123
Lundgren, Carl, 153
Macdonald, Ross, 238, 240-245, 249-259
Malta (country), 58, 83
Maltese falcon (antiquity), 22, 37, 59, 62-64, 72, 79, 82-85, 87-89, 198-199, 202-204, 206-207, 239
The Maltese Falcon (novel), 22-23, 26, 28-30, 37, 48, 84, 87, 90
Malvern, Marcus, 139-140, 152, 154, 210
Malvern, Ted, 151-159, 192-193
Man in the Shadows (novel), 185
Marlowe, Philip, 148, 189-191, 193, 196, 210-214, 234-236, 240-244, 249-256, 258-259, 263
Mars, Eddie, 202-203, 207, 210-211, 224, 232-233, 250-251
Marty, Joe, 108
Megaron Hotel (Heraklion, Crete), 206
Mesarvey, Joe, 128, 139, 143, 146,

150, 162, 202-204
Millar, Annie, 24, 39-41, 73, 91
Millar, John Macdonald, 12, 24, 28, 38-42, 56, 62, 70-78, 80-81, 91, 265
  birth, 12
Millar, Kenneth, 42, 265
Mohamet (prophet), 132
Monahan, Dixie, 61
Moore, Colleen, 132
Musso & Frank Grill (restaurant), 108
My Lady Friends (play), 12
Nagasaki, Japan (destruction of), 263
New York, New York, 44, 60, 170, 205
  Coney Island, 194
nickelodeon, 12, 146
No, No, Nanette (musical), 182
Northcott, Gordon Stewart, 110
Northcott, Sanford, 110
Northcott, Sarah Louise, 110
notebook, 52-55, 65-69, 73-78, 85, 98-103, 105-107, 111-117, 120-123, 126-127, 130-132, 135-136, 143-147, 149-150, 154, 159-169, 175-181, 183-185, 188-197, 199, 210-217, 226-236
O'Mara Investigations, 207, 231
O'Shaughnessy, Brigid, 28, 31, 33, 48
Outlaws on the Run (film), 230
Pabst, G. W., 187
Pacific Coast Highway, 220
Pacoima, California, 94
Paducah, Kentucky, 94
Pandora's Box (film), 187
Parsons, Louella, 247
Pascal, Cissy, 44-45, 173-174, 191-192, 239
Pascal, Julian, 44-46, 80, 170, 173-179, 181-185, 187-193, 213, 216, 238-239, 247-248
Petronius, Gaius (Gaius Petronius Arbiter), 123
Philadelphia, Pennsylvania, 94

Pierce, Charles, 31
Pierce Motors, 31
Pinkerton, Allan, 16
Pinkerton National Detective Agency, 14-19, 32-34, 36, 46, 50, 56, 67, 80, 153
Piraeus, Greece, 206
Polhaus, Tom, 68
Pomona, California, 94
Prohibition (Eighteenth Amendment, U.S. Constitution), 12
Puddler, (*see* Yeager, Lash)
"Putting on the Ritz" (song), 212
Queen Elizabeth Hospital for Incurables (Toronto, Canada), 265
Regina (province of Canada), 110
Reilly Motor Company, 34-36
Reilly, Penelope, 34-36
Reilly, Stanley, 32-36, 271
Richman, Harry, 212
R. M. S. Aquitania (ocean liner), 206
R. M. S. Lusitania (ocean liner), 34
Robinson, Jack, 137
Roosevelt, Franklin Delano, 12
Roosevelt Hotel (Los Angeles, California), 95, 98, 110, 115, 125-126, 130, 134-135, 139, 149, 154, 156-157, 175, 215
Ruth, George Herman, Jr. (Babe), 12, 145, 231
Salvation Army, 157
Sampson, Penelope (*also see* Archer, Iva, *also see* Goodbody, Iva), 23-24, 224, 263, 272
Sampson, Ralph, 24, 40, 206, 222-224, 231, 248, 263
San Diego, California, 17, 39, 225
San Francisco Bay, 14-15, 18, 52, 60, 210
San Francisco, California, 12-13, 15-16, 18, 20, 24-27, 35-36, 40-41, 43-45, 57, 85, 91, 104, 138, 170, 174, 188, 194, 199, 202-203, 207, 210, 222-223, 238

284 INDEX

Barbary Coast (neighborhood of), 23, 52, 116, 222-223
Tenderloin (neighborhood of), 116
Santa Monica Bay, 140
Santa Monica, California, 128, 139-141, 152-154, 185, 188, 207, 220, 226, 249, 254
Santa Teresa, California, 23, 39-40, 129, 151, 211, 218-225, 227-229, 232, 239, 248, 250-251, 262
    earthquake (1925), 219
Santa Ynez Mountains, 220
Sawyer, Tom (fictional character), 162
Seattle, Washington, 17, 36
Security First National (bank), 58
Security Trust Building, 137, 148, 157
shadow, 11-265
Sir Francis Drake Hotel, 78, 84, 88
Solomon (Biblical king), 130, 229
South Basin Oil Company, 44-45, 80, 87, 170, 172-175, 190, 198, 203, 206-207, 210, 238-239, 244, 246-248, 259, 271-272
Spade, Sam (fictional character), 22, 28-32, 48
Spanish-American War, 172, 224
    Battle of San Juan Hill, 224
Spice Islands, 202
Spokane, Washington, 19, 31-35
Spreckels, Alma, 80
Stanford, Leland, Jr., 219
Stanley Rose Bookshop, 98
Steiner, Harold Hardwicke, 95-97, 99, 105-106, 116-117, 120-124, 143-145, 147, 150, 154, 169, 174-180, 201, 203, 209, 211-212, 216
Sternwood, Carmen, 46-47, 57-58, 62-64, 71, 80, 87, 89, 200-203, 205-207, 262-263
Sternwood, Norris (General), 45-46, 57-58, 62, 80-81, 86, 88-89, 169-178, 180, 198, 200-201, 205-207, 212, 223-225, 246-247, 252, 262-264
Sternwood, Penelope Ann, 224
Sternwood, Vivian, 205, 262
St. Francis Hotel (see Hotel St. Francis)
streetcar, 40, 73-74, 98, 107, 117, 125, 157, 182, 188, 190, 209, 240, 243, 262, 272
Tacoma Tribune, 33
Tacoma, Washington, 17, 30, 33-34
Taj Mahal, 227
Taylor, Owen, 174, 206, 238-245, 249-259
The Thin Man (novel), 264
Thursby, Floyd, 48, 84, 88, 206, 238
Toronto, Canada, 265
Troy, Dwight (MD), 40
tuberculosis, 14, 17
Tweed, William (Boss), 130
United States Army, 14, 17-18, 27, 34, 223
Valentino, Rudolph, 135
Vancouver, B. C., 39
Venice Beach, California, 153
Veracruz, Mexico, 36
Walgreen, L. D., 13
Wallace, Dan, 49-64, 70-78, 80, 84-85, 88-89, 206, 238
Warner-Pacific Studio, 132
Whitley, H. J., 171, 218
The Wild Piano (restaurant), 98, 100
Wilson, William, 262
Wonderley, Carmen, 47-50, 57, 60, 62-64, 70-78, 80, 87, 90
World War I, 11-12, 14, 17, 35-36
Wright, Orville, 12
Wright, Wilbur, 12
Yeager, Lash (Puddler), 145, 162-164, 167-168, 190, 192-193, 203-204, 211, 233
Ziegfeld, Florenz, 223
Ziegfeld Follies, 23-24, 223, 272
"Zigzags of Treachery" (story), 19

ABOUT THE EDITOR

Gabriel Blackwell is the author of *Critique of Pure Reason*. He lives in Portland, OR with his wife, Jessica.

Made in the USA
San Bernardino, CA
06 June 2014